WRAPPED IN RED

ALANA I. CAPRIA

MONTAG

Dedication

To my rabbits, Drama and Cassi. I'll miss you until we meet at the
Rainbow Bridge.

To my husband, Eddie. Thank you for your unconditional love
and support.

To my mom, Ana. You're the strongest woman I know.

PART ONE

MY DISORDER

Sleeping Beauty on a Bed of Needles

Sleeping Beauty swallows five spools of thread and a spindle against her parents' orders. It takes three boxes of sleeping pills a night to close her eyes. The fairies tire of sewing her eyelashes down. Sleeping Beauty is allergic to glue in all forms. The fairies ply her with poisoned lemons but Sleeping Beauty refuses to bite. [The pith is too bitter,] she says as she plays her grandmother's spindle like a harp. A braid of hair stolen from her former best friend is sewn down against her scalp. Maybe the hair isn't twenty thousand miles long but Sleeping Beauty does what she can with the length she has. It is head to toe and enough to make men look in her direction. Give her a pair of glass slippers and there has never been a more beautiful princess. She has no problem spitting up swallowed needles to get the guy. They all like the prick of her touch. Some men prefer bleeding when it comes to love. The men carry a little wound from every

morning glory.

woman they've ever met. To show them how serious she
is Sleeping Beauty has the flesh of her stomach replaced
with a pane of glass. She strips naked and lets them
see how the stomach acid works the scissors' handles
around a spool of string. By twisting her torso, she can
force her stomach to knot the thread into bows. It takes
talent and dedication to the art of mocking her pitfalls.
Sometimes the men are a little too careful around her.
They think that every sharp object will make her faint.
[No knives for her. No razor blades,] they say. They'll let
her starve and go hairy instead. She feels feeble. With
the men away, Sleeping Beauty sits alone in her boudoir
and practices cutting her arm muscles with the tip of a
steak knife. Nothing makes her sleep. She keeps the pin
cushion for another day, when the men snore in her ear.

The first of the men raped her. She was left with several children just sitting around. She didn't know what to
do with them. Eventually she let the servants place the
children in a bricked-up bath. Anything that wouldn't
disturb her sleep. After that Sleeping Beauty decided
to practice her youth group's motto of 'be prepared'.
She kept an assortment of needles in her back pockets
so that as soon as her fingers settled upon the spindle,
she could pull one out and hold it threateningly. No man
wanted to kiss a princess who might jab him in the eye
with a sewing needle. Sleeping Beauty was that kind of
girl. Sure, there were a few dozen men who wanted to

experience that element of danger but she was prepared. When they leaned in too close, they got pricked in the face. She never saw them cry but her hands were wet for days afterwards. It taught the men several things. Number one was that sleeping princesses had to give permission for a kiss. The second was that a needle should never be taken lightly. The third was that ocular injuries take years to heal. Maybe the fairies got angry with her behavior. They wanted a princess who was a model of self-control. Instead, they got Sleeping Beauty who would have preferred a long, sharp needle to an engagement ring. Let the men come with their swords and knives. She had better tools. Every woman knew how to use a needle. The men thought nothing of the silver slivers until the tips pushed into their eye lids as they bent to kiss her. They bled as much by the tip of the needle as by any other sharp weapon. Sleeping Beauty always knew to put her sewing skills to good use. Even if she wasn't their favorite, the fairies had taught her very well.

Sleeping Beauty has a Medusa wig. All those albino snakes make her itch. [There is itching powder in my wig,] she accuses the princes assembled around her. They paint her skin blue and swathe her bedroom in a deep rose fabric. [You have never looked lovelier,] the princes say. They fall to their knees and kiss her hands finger by finger. Despite the discomfort, she loves the wig. The snake tongues embed in her scalp and stay rooted despite any twisting she might do in her sleep. Their mouths bite her. She slaps the snakes to teach proper behavior. Still, the snakes come in handy. When the princes get too close and Sleeping Beauty wants to tie her legs together, the snakes rear back and bite their faces. She cannot turn men to stone but to ice. To fire. To hay. She can melt them or freeze them. She can set them on fire and warm her hands. Sleeping Beauty walks around with a mourning gown on. It was the same gown her grandmother wore when she decided to become an evil witch in a parsley-covered tower. Hence, Rapunzel became her best friend. Hence, Sleeping Beauty stole the coveted hair away and used the spindle to sew the long locks onto her scalp. [You make me sleep,] Sleeping Beauty told Rapunzel during family gatherings. Sleeping Beauty knows how to stitch thread through her fingernails. The trick is painful but Sleeping Beauty likes the look of golden string weaving through enamel. The princes like it, too. Little do the princes know that the snakes use the thread as chains to pull themselves across Sleeping Beauty's delicate hands. The princes touch her wrists and the snakes bite. Sleeping Beauty breathes fire. She burns the princes. Ember piles assemble around her bed.

As a gift for her sweet sixteen, the Snow White witch gives Sleeping Beauty an inversion mirror. Sleeping Beauty looks into the glass and sees herself as a negative image with the lightest areas of her face appearing darkest and the darkest areas appearing lightest. As she gazes upon herself in the birthday mirror, she holds a needle in both hands. Snow White should have known to keep a needle in her apple. That would have been enough to keep the ill-smelling dwarfs at bay and teach wandering gentlemen to let glass coffins be. Every spindle has a point. The king shouldn't be so worried about spindles and sleep. The evil witch only wanted to prove a point. Sleeping Beauty keeps the needles in a vase beside her bed. She tests each point on the front of her teeth. She kisses each on the eye. She wraps the shafts with a strand of her hair. [Take that,] she says when the men battle ivy spines to reach her. She throws the needles at them as they creep up the stairs towards her. The needles cut what the thorns can't. She sticks needles pointed side up through the mattress. The men bleed when they lean onto the mattress to kiss her. Sleeping Beauty has an affection for sanguine fluids. She holds the drops of blood from the men between two fingers until they clot fully. She smears a dot of clotted blood across every nail and pushes the needle point into the center. The goal is to keep the bubble from bursting. It is not easy to do. The borders of the blood bubbles constantly move, threatening to spill over. But Sleeping Beauty knows how to manipulate spindles and blood. She has pricked enough fingers and fallen asleep enough times. All that practice makes her a professional. She can keep a needle in place for three days before the bubble even makes a ripple. Let any other princess lay claim to that. Sleeping Beauty knows they can't.

Sleeping Beauty isn't the type of girl who is afraid to walk down school hallways with a knife in her back pocket. A blade gives her a sense of security. Just like the time she pretended she had miles of hair and let men climb the braids. They got half way up before she let the hair fall, and with it the men to their death. So Sleeping Beauty has a love affair with a flower adorned chair with a golden needle. It is decorated with smoky orbs and glittering leaves. It invites her to take a seat. Take a load off. Let her butt rest awhile. It is tempting. Still, there is a needle stuck in the cushion resting upon the seat and she can't look past that point. She always touches the chair at the same moment the wash begins. Then the floor shakes. The chair shakes. She shakes. It is a hard lesson. Steadiness is key in all affairs of a fresh needle. A rusty needle is more forgiving than a golden needle. The point is not as sharp. It can take a few more beatings. It can be pushed through its breaking point. Inevitably, it will break. The spindle will break. Sleeping Beauty will break, as will all her friends in the princess brigade. Without needles to protect them, they all break in the hands of men, like dolls. Ripped apart and thrown away. Too many have children without ever knowing the fathers. Too many find out later that the fathers already had wives they had no intention of leaving. Sleeping Beauty had to deal with thirteen men just like that. They all promised her stars but refused to give her a ring. They could have given her a spindle with a magical needle. Then, once pricked, she could have slept the labors off and woken up after the kids were born, grown, and gone away. From her window in the castle she sees them from time to time, her children, standing in the marketplace. A few are prostitutes, some are beggars sick with the plague, and the rest are wives beaten by their men and circumstance. She can't help their lives.

Hanging in the great hall, there are about five thousand pictures of her with the same pose and the same smile, wearing five thousand different dresses, just leaning against a wall. Every picture has the same wall in it. The photographer told her not to think. Instead she was told to smile politely and stare blankly into space. [You are a perfect princess,] he said. [You are perfect in every way, never change.] Sleeping Beauty had an obsession with golden roses back then. Now, after her uterus has dilated and swelled repeatedly with her many children, her interests have turned more towards golden orbs and ratios. She knows math. There is only a specific amount of times hair can wind around a spindle. The numbers change slightly when dealing with Rapunzel's hair but that is expected. Some people have miles-long hair and

others do not. Then again, some people have a life re-
volving around a spindle and others choose a basket of
parsley. Sleeping Beauty also learns the importance of
meat. She used to love roasted turkey legs and mashed
potatoes but time has taught her that the best meats are
the ones provided so generously by her suitors. A bit of
their genitals roasted with a side salad or parsley. A fillet
of open rib. A taste of braised buttocks with her mashed
potatoes. She can eat those men for days. Of course, the
parents shun such behavior. [No daughter of ours will
resort to cannibalism], the almighty king says and Sleeping Beauty laughs and throws him an apple. Maybe it
is Snow White's apple, maybe not. Of course, there is a
needle and thorn in it. Unlike Snow White, she never
forgets to booby trap her apples. She pricks her thumbs
on both and smiles smugly before fainting dead in the
throne room. It takes seventeen servants to carry her up
the thousand steps to her bedroom. It doesn't help that
the suitors' meat makes her a little heavier around the
middle. She likes how the curves make her look in the
magic mirror.

A few suitors try spearing her but Sleeping Beauty
has been stabbing herself for years. She regularly keeps
needles poking through her quilted waistcoat. It is an
important reminder of what keeps her awake and what
doesn't. There are even needles in her hair. Once a
year, she lets the fairies push thin needles into the flesh

around her eyes. During these times she willingly goes blind while her eye balls come out of their sockets. Her eyes move around her body and she sees different parts of herself. Up her nose. Down her mouth. Around her throat. Into her ears. Down her back. Between her legs. She learns about her body. At those times, she keeps a veil over her face and waits for the suitors. They touch her body lovingly, thinking that without her eyes, she must be asleep. Her eyes travel across their backs, up and over their shoulders and watch intently as the men make love to her. It is strange to watch. She rarely feels excited by the act. As soon as they have finished, her eyes focus on the faces so she can watch their shock as her sleepless hands rise up for the unveiling of her needle-filled eye sockets. Much to her delight, nearly every suitor screams. Several scream so loudly that they lose their voices. A few suffer snapped throats. However, her favorites are the ones who sit silently, mouths hanging open, expressions blank. She gently touches the silent ones on the thigh, then the throat. She kisses their shoulders. She rubs their arms. With her eyes perched on her shoulders, she leads them to an iron bathtub where she drains them with the needles she pulls free of her jeweled bodice. Stripping naked, she climbs into the tub with them, eats from their liver, and drinks from their wrists. [But I came here to save you,] some of the suitors have said. [And here you have saved me, and now after sleeping for a hundred years I am hungry,] she answers.

At balls, her parents always said, [Sleeping Beauty, do not pretend to be so dangerous. It is not right. No man wants that. You will be alone forever.] She never listened. Instead, she pierced her nipples with foot-long needles and wore the tips on the outside of her dress. It was a conversation piece. Every suitor wanted to know why she mutilated her body. Every suitor wanted to be the one who might get the chance to pull the needles out. Maybe even lick the warm holes left behind. Instead, once she guided these suitors away from the dance floor, Sleeping Beauty chopped their hands off. She used the meat for a stew she fed her parents on their wedding anniversary. [Such meat,] the queen said, sampling. [It's suitors,] Sleeping Beauty said and pricked the spindle. Away she fell, to sleep for one hundred years while life continued around her without aging. The fairies poked needles through her body while she slept. It was their job to turn her into a pin cushion. A needle stuck out of every vital organ. A needle in each cardiovascular ventricle. A needle at the starting point of every vein. A needle to separate skin layers. The youngest fairy tied a ribbon onto the needles she pushed in. They booby-trapped the halls with needles. A piece of metal between every tile and in every doorknob. No suitor could get through without being stabbed at least once. When she woke up, she ate her first meal of suitor au jus, one of the lucky few to make it through the castle halls and find her sleeping body. After she was full, Sleeping Beauty wandered down the hallway and licked the point of every needle clean. She tasted from all the suitors she had missed. Among the many dead she saw what she couldn't.

Sleeping Beauty vomited up stones to cover the palace. She was tired of the thorns. She always pricked her fingers when she woke up. She didn't mind the threat of stubbing her toes as long as no blood was drawn. So rock faces grew around her. She looked out of her bedroom window and saw layered burgundy granite encircling the castle. Relieved, she sat on the bed. She heard metallic scrapings against the rock. Looking out again, she saw suitors climbing the wall. They called to her. [Rapunzel,] they screamed. She broke through the glass. [My name is Sleeping Beauty,] she hissed and caused the layered rocks to fall. Evil fairies came to pick apart the crushed bodies. Sleeping Beauty sat with them, silently eating bits of suitor leg matter. She settled on devouring the red toes. They were bony but plump and they were plentiful.

With her dagger points, Sleeping Beauty was always prepared for dragons as well as the rapists. Her favorite was the man who left her pregnant, then returned to feed her. He let her drink from the palm of his hand while their children pulled at her pierced nipples. His wife, a princess from another land, had followed him. She wanted Sleeping Beauty to mount a pyre and burn to atone for the illegitimate children. Wielding a broad sword, the princess swore an epic battle between princess and queen, rape victim and rightful wife. Sleeping Beauty defended herself, needles in hand. Then, once the pyre had been set, the suitor turned on his wife and burnt her instead. He turned to Sleeping Beauty for comfort. He grabbed her wrists. [Will you marry me,] the suitor asked. [I love only you.] Sleeping Beauty grabbed their children and pushed them out the window. [There is no need for that,] she said as she pushed him away and out the window too. He crashed to the ground and crawled through the ivy on his belly, dragging his broken limbs behind. He cried up to her, [You are perfect for me. Do not forsake me.] Sleeping Beauty looked down and watched his blood water the roses. [You are doing a wonderful job,] she called to him. [Don't stop now.] Encouraged, he dragged himself up the thousand steps to her boudoir and sobbed, begging at her feet, [Please love me.] She kicked his shoulders out. [You will be a very rich meal,] she said. [And for that I will always be grateful.] She devoured him in three bites. Of all her suitors, Sleeping Beauty misses that suitor from time to time. She might have kept him strung up in the bathtub and eaten a little piece of him every day for as long as he lasted. But when she is asleep, her hunger gets away from her. Someone puts meat in her mouth and she dreams as she chews.

Sleeping Beauty hides in closets to listen to the suitors telling stories while running up the one thousand steps. Silently she follows behind them past the landings. [She is a ghost,] they tell one another. [She carries needles in her bouquet and blends into walls.] Sleeping Beauty laughs at the reference. She loves the idea of being a ghost. Her needles clink together in her hands. She fastens ribbons around their necks, then silently, like a ghost, she retraces her steps down the stairs. From where she left them, strangling in ribbons, she trails gasoline after her. At the bottom of the flight, she lights a match and turns away. The stairs alight. But it is okay because the stairs are made of stone. A spark lights her hair on fire but she can afford to go bald. She doesn't rely on her hair for nourishment. All she needs is a spindle and poisoned wheel. Above her, the men scream. She walks into the garden and stands beneath her bedroom window. The suitors, covered in flames, leap out and fall into her unhinged mouth. She swallows them like a snake, asphyxiating their burned bodies with the pressure of her throat. [Why,] the stronger one asks as he squeezes his way out. Sleeping Beauty shows him her hands covered with needle pricks. [I am tired of falling asleep,] she says as she swallows him down. She always feels a little remorse for the handsome ones but not enough to let them out of her mouth. She is too hungry for that. Her children dot the countryside. They wave at her in recognition as they come to the castle, but she doesn't know their names. Still she eats the men who try impregnating her again. She is tired of waking up hungry, pregnant, and with children to feed. It isn't the sex that bothers her. It is the men's desire for her to bear their children against her will. It is that the men, the suitors, the princes, all feel entitled to fill her with their bodies but never with food. This happens while she sleeps for one hundred years. It's only fair that she devours them in return.

Rapunzel Lives Again – Act One

When Rapunzel spilled her hair out of the tower, every-thing drowned. Her roots were many different colors. The ends were dyed red with the witch's menstrual fluid. The prince looked at her and he turned red, too. The scarlet thickness came out of his eyes and wet the floor. Rapunzel preferred being a brunette but the witch kept the hair dye in a safe. [Sorry, my dear,] she said, prepar-ing red-dye bottles. [I like you better as a ginger.] Rapun-zel cried for four days, then took a razor to her scalp. A few times, the prince poured bleach onto her head. [You would be a nice blonde,] he said, massaging her stubbly hair follicles. Rapunzel unhooked her wig and threw it out the window. [Fetch,] she said and pushed him out after it. That was just how it was. Everyone wanted to change the princess. It all started with her mother's hun-ger for herbs. Rapunzel was lucky she had avoided grow-ing a leaf as a face. Though, if it had been a brilliant red, she might have been able to stand it.

Sleeping Beauty wore a fish head to sleep. Marine fangs, spiked dorsal fins, and gills chased suitors away. A few came with fishing hooks. They wanted to catch a big one. Her lure-headed tongue caught the bait and held on. This happened whenever she got her period. But the men never came to clean her up, which is what she needed. They came to gut her mouth with their rods and poles. It was hard for her to avoid nightmares. Every dream involved a scene of her swallowing a rubber worm flavored with bacon. Sleeping Beauty couldn't stand porcine products. They made her neck bloat. The few men not armed with rods came to look at her. The vacancy of her eyes was scary. They touched her fangs gently, afraid she would bite. These men wished she had layers of scales to cover her nudity. A fish head and naked breasts were not known for their miscegenation. Surprisingly, it lacked a certain arousal. They much preferred the opposite.

Small red hooded things lived in the forest below. They kept felt capes fastened over their long ears. They smelled wolves easily. The predator stench was ubiquitous among the acorns. The stronger the peanut stench, the faster the females ran. Naked men waited for them in the clearing. From under their hoods, the girls stared at their erect genitals. [What would we even do with that,] they asked. They kept their hands in their baskets, floating just above the knife. The men snickered and grabbed the girls' adolescent breasts. [You will put it in you,] they said. Feigning reluctance, the girls pulled their hoods lower and got on their knees. The men felt around for the girls' lips. They didn't mind the bit of hair above the mouth. They stuck their penises in and waited for the suckle. Their hands pushed the hoods back. That is when they saw the tiny smiling wolf heads and the tender penises stuck between jaws lined with sharp teeth.

Finally old Lady Rapunzel died. It was her own fault. All those years of growing her hair out caused her to wither and die. The witch scraped the Rapunzel pancake off the ground and ate it. No more Rapunzel. It was sad to see her go. She had been beautiful up until the end. Shed of her skin, she had turned into a skeleton, fingers clasped together and a slit going up the front of her dress. Finally she was truly beautiful. She let anyone see her genitals, opening her dress as she walked, and spreading her legs as she sat. The hair coming off of them was silken and brushed along the floor. She kept the strands braided so she could walk easily. Her husband pleasured her orally and jokingly she choked him with the pubic hair braids, wrapping them around his neck and pulling tight. Her once-red face shriveled up. She became a grayish raisin stuck to her skull. To some, her newly skeletal body was hideous. Every small boy was kissed with a creaking noise. Every little girl was caressed with a slurp.

But still her husband loved her. He was a simple man.

One thing that Rapunzel knew to be true is that oceans turn red when they die. Their deaths are always by suicide. No ocean is ever killed. Nothing is that powerful. Some girls were shunned and so the mermaids dropped them to the bottom of the sea. Goodbye, fish women. Goodbye. Like the girls living on the ship bow. They watched their lovers marry other women. But heartbreak didn't kill all. For one, it was her time of the month when her lover married another woman. Her uterus dropped out of her. It was a torturous emptying. Her body turned inside out so she stabbed her chest to prevent transforming into a squid. Everyone would have hacked her limbs off anyway. No man broke his boat on a rock jetty to kiss a parrot-beaked mermaid. So the girl stabbed herself and dropped into an abyss. She turned into red foam. The jellied eggs impregnated everything they touched. All the animals in the sea had merbabies. This Rapunzel knew.

Sleeping Beauty told Rapunzel about Hansel and Gretel. Once in the oven, Hansel's cooked face turned bright red. The cheeks looked to be slicked with sugar and food coloring. It was a dish publicized as fake Asian takeout. But it was just a boy. The witch stared proudly at the apple adorned fellow and bit off his roasted ear. His skin was seasoned with a good amount of sea salt. The witch hadn't bothered cooking the girl. Her bones were too skinny. The witch had known this all along. No twigs could fool her. Even with her bad eyesight she knew that it was the boy who was the one with all the fat. Gretel sat at the head of the table. She kept the fork and knife in her tiny fists. The witch served the girl a taste of her brother's backside. Gretel dressed the meat with gravy. [He has never tasted so delicious,] Gretel said, alluding to the secret things that happened when she and the boy were alone in the parental cottage. She finished three heaping dishes of his face. She kept asking for more. For dessert, she was served a flaming bowl of Hansel's sugared testicles soaked in brandy. The skin dumplings had a caramel crust Gretel broke through. She and the witch sighed over the meal. They hoped that there would be others. Then they kissed. If only her parents could see her now. She was happy, like she had always dreamt she would be.

Red allergies cut the girls' eyes. Rapunzel rubbed her eyes until her irises fell out. Sleeping Beauty touched her pupils and they bit her fingertips. No one could see straight. A fine red powder settled on the windowsills. The girls breathed the dust in. [Is it only the dust of skeletons,] they asked. [What about the ash of princes? That is what we want.] They dragged their tongues along the wood-grain. The dust tasted acidic. [A rich red wine,] Sleeping Beauty muttered and pulled a flask out of her pillow. She drank a body's worth of vinegar. Eventually, servants came to put the eyes back together. Sleeping Beauty fell asleep each time a needle touched her. The servants used a pair of scissors on Rapunzel and cut off her hair under the guise of it being an accident. Both girls were left on the ground for rats to find. When they did, they curled up together with their vinegar breath.

When Rapunzel spilled the red waste hanging onto her skeletal ribs, she sickened. The witch hung her emaciated frame out the window. It was so the prince could climb the tower faster. From a distance, it still appeared that the girl had curves. But that was just her hair. He reached her and starving Rapunzel pulled him in. She ate him quickly. Red smeared her face. The witch watched curiously as she picked up the discarded bones. Together they boiled the bones in a soup for thirteen days until the water thickened. Rapunzel lingered around the fire. She cooked her hands with the residual heat. The prince's skull rolled around the room. He knocked against Rapunzel's ankles. She leaned down and stroked his hair as he kissed her toes. [Where is your hair,] he asked. [You looked so beautiful with long hair.] She lifted the skull and shoved it into her pelvis. She held him there, gasping from breath, for her pleasure.

The Trials and Tribulations of Little Red - Act One

Little Red carved the wolf's pelt. She wanted a tail for the back of her hood. The wolf whimpered beneath the knife. Grandmother watched closely. [Do not cut yourself,] the old woman cautioned. Little red's hands were coated with blood. She licked each finger separately, then held the thumbs beneath the wolf's nose. He licked the nails miserably. His blood had a metallic taste that ruined his appetite. Little Red giggled and shoved his mouth into hers. She slurped the fur around his snout and pulled back his black lips with her tongue. The wolf showed her his teeth. Red pulled her cheeks back to bare her own. They were stubbled with red matter. Her breath smelled like a slaughterhouse. [All the better to eat you with,] she snarled.

Tailless, but without fury or vengeance, the wolf tore the little girl in half to see what was stuffed inside. [I am curious if you have ever been rolled into raw pasta dough,] the wolf said, parting her intestines and scooping digested meat from their centers. He yanked her red hood off and fitted his hands into the soft temple space above her ears, pushing aside nerve endings and tiny glass shards. [You are like a building in there,] the wolf whispered, his elbows touching the outer rim of her flesh. The girl batted her eyes helplessly. Her tongue lolled around in her mouth. The wolf pushed farther into her skull. The girl giggled and wagged her genitalia in front of him. It moved up and down, tickling the wolf's inner thighs. [I am not done dying,] she whispered. She swallowed and her bones hardened. Her bones pressed back against the wolf's paws. They crushed his wrists. Red swallowed repeatedly, gasping in between mouthfuls of air. [Now it is my turn to dissect you,] she said and she flipped the salivating wolf around. Mounting him from behind caused him to howl in delight.

Little Red was more afraid of her incestuous grandmother than the wolf that came to join her nightly in her bedroom. [Have you had a hard day in the forest,] the girl asked, pulling the burrs and thorns from the wolf's gray fur. He licked the red tufts caught between his teeth before answering. [I had a lucky day. At first there was just one lonely girl walking alone through the woods, then when I thought that there would be no more, there were three. I ate them all. Split me open for your dinner,] he said, sprawling across the bed. Red took an ax and cut just below the navel. She pulled the half-digested meat out and cooked it in a sauce made of her favorite white wine; fresh ground pepper, and smoked paprika. In the morning, the wolf went back into the trees and Red reluctantly set off for her grandmother's house. She walked quickly, dragging the wolf's cooked wares in her basket. The grandmother answered the door in a red lacy negligee. [I thought you would never arrive,] she breathed into the girl's neck. Without warning, as was usual, she pushed Red onto the kitchen table. Grandmother ate from Red's chest, groin, and stomach before the girl managed to push her away and sprint home, intestines dragging behind her.

When the wolf found Red, she was bluer in color than pink. The wolf threw himself onto her open casket, mourning her cold hands and lack of hood. [Why is there no cape? The cape is the only way we recognize her,] the wolf howled, biting the girl's bloody grandmother. The old woman stood grinning beside the little girl's body. She wore a wolf teeth chain around her neck and whipped her body to one side, striking his cheek with the sharp ends. A plastic bag cradled Red's head. It created a synthetic halo around her head. The more the wolf watched, the fleshier the bag became, as if it were a part of her. There were bear bites around Red's hard pale neck. The marks were deep and purplish. The wolf leaned so close, his muzzle flattened against her body.

[A bear,] he whispered. [Of all the things you could leave me for, a bear?] The wolf clawed at his mouth in despair. Inconsolable he threw the casket over, knocking Red out. She rolled out of the casket, landing on her stomach. The back of her head was a cavernous hole. There was no brain. In the woods, her bear lover played with her cortex, her intestines fashionably draped around his thick fur neck.

They covered the girl in a red hood to hide her monstrous face. Her skin was puckered leather and her jaws were twisted. Because of this, she could not speak. Instead, she moaned and grunted her likes and dislikes, knocking her head against the walls until her forehead splintered enough to reveal the pulsing gray matter beneath. The red hood was thought to protect those gaps in her skull from infection and disease. They tied the hooded girl to an oak tree and left her resting against the roots in hopes that something would end her suffering. Instead, the wolf arrived. It sniffed her musty groin, then stuck its cold wet nose against her mouth. The red-hooded girl shifted her massive bottom jaw and scraped the fur from the wolf's head. The wolf howled in pleasure and bit her neck. The girl growled back. She strained against the ropes, twisting in the loops and cutting her skin against the rough tree trunk, overcome by pleasure. [How ugly,] the wolf whispered, parting the cracked folds of her hood to reveal the throbbing amniotic tissue tucked between her legs. The wolf sliced her head off her shoulders. A clutter of spiders scattered out of her. It was the first time he had known love.

Little Red was covered in hair and yarn and no matter how often the wolf searched, he could not find her. The beast parted curls but was unable to remove her. He yanked pigtails but there were no hands inside. The wolf found coils of yarn and unwound each one in the hopes that the girl would come barreling out. But still, there was no little red. So he sat in her picnic basket, hoping she would come and lift him. But the wicker only stayed on the forest path's dirt. The wolf howled for the grandmother, then peeked into her kitchen window. He saw the old woman sprawled on the kitchen table, long locks of hair stretching over her eyes and mouth, tying her to the table legs. The wolf went away. He took a razor blade to his legs and shaved the fur off. The tufts fell, coloring the ground dark gray. Little Red moaned in her hair nest. She threw up follicles and roots. The wolf shaved his paws. He cut the hair from his face. The nude wolf curled up to the girl's hair and slept as close to her as he could. He knew she was in there somewhere.

Then one day, a girl who reminded the wolf of Red menstruated in front of him. He suffered to see the amount of blood pouring out of her. When the girl closed her eyes in the midst of an abdominal cramp, the wolf stuck his paws in the red puddles and skimmed the uterine tissue off the top. He smeared the chunks on his fur and howled three times before running away. Soon thereafter the wolf brought the girl meat. It was the only thing that he remembered how to do. He pulled grandma hides to her, the bodies newly killed and still warm to the touch. The girl ate from the chest plates and shoulder blades. She tore into the muscle. The chops hung from her mouth. They draped over her neck. The wolf licked the juices running off the gristle. His new Little Red groaned and squeezed her abdomen tight. Her womb slipped out of her. It smelled strongly of saline air. The wolf ate his tail. He ran around in circles, slipping in her juices. Then the girl, whom he did not recognize, turned and cut the wolf with the ax of her tongue. [I am not to blame for my body's starving fertility,] she said. [It is not my fault.]

This new red-hooded girl removed her face and the wolf stared into the pulpy flesh. [What is this massacre,] the canis lupus asked, pressing its paws into the meat. The girl opened her mouth and laughed shortly. [I am just a piece of meat cloaked in a red hood,] she gasped and broke a mirror with her head. A mirror she was told was magic. She lifted away from the glass. Muscle juices streaked the glass. The wolf lifted her face. He held the flaps of flesh to his muzzle. [I can be you if I stitch this to myself,] the wolf whispered to her. The girl turned away from him. She got on her hands and knees and devoured the dirt. Rocks fell from her mouth. Her tongue cracked apart. The wolf forced the red-hooded girl's face over his own. He stretched the skin and smoothed it over his ears. He tucked his fur in. He stood on his back legs and leaned over her. She looked up. Her bulging eyes rolled around several times before focusing on him. [How did I get over there when I am still here,] she asked, sneezing.

When the wolf demanded meat, the red-hooded girl cut into her thighs and gave him all the muscle she could pull out with her curved nails. He ate more than she could produce and she was forced to slice open her bone and give him the buttered marrow stored within. The wolf groaned in hunger as he slurped the bone cream she offered him. The wolf grabbed her arms and bit into the biceps, tearing the meat apart. The girl poured water over the wounds to nurse them. She slathered them with lemongrass and waited for her cells to replicate. With nothing left to eat, the wolf starved for the next meal. The girl crawled across the forest floor to her grandmother's house. She screamed. The grandmother came out. The girl killed her with an ax. [I am sorry for this murder,] the girl said as she dragged the grandmother back to the wolf. He lay on his back, starving. His bones showed through his mangy fur. The girl pushed the grandmother to him. [Do what you need to,] she said and he stripped off the old woman's clothes to get at the soft white meat.

The girl was just a pile of straw left in a field for the wolf to find. He sniffed the green edges and nuzzled up to the bundle. [I am curious to know what you are,] the wolf said. He spoke in a low voice, trying to seduce the hay into moving but the pile stayed still. The wolf tickled the straw with his tail. A red cape poked out of the top. It caught the breeze and flapped. The wolf watched the red wave. He salivated. His spittle dripped over the hay, wetting the wheat until it softened and drooped. [What are you doing,] the wolf shouted. He cradled the wilting straw. He rubbed his face against the material and tiny plant burs stuck to his cheeks. [I would die for you,] the wolf said. He climbed up the pile. The wolf pulled the red cape around his stomach and legs. [I am bleeding now,] he marveled. The wolf knocked his teeth against his claws to make a spark. He directed the flame at the hay. The straw caught fire. [We'll die together, then we'll be married,] the wolf said, burning.

Rapunzel and the Knife – Act Two

Twice a day, Rapunzel would rip out her hair and grow a new braid. The rest of the day was spent waiting with her head in a bathtub filled with peroxide. It took hours for the black roots to develop the golden hue she was famous for. [You take too long,] the ogre said, crawling in and out of Rapunzel's favorite mirror but the princess simply wrung her wet hair into a garbage can. Rapunzel did what it took for the men to continue scaling the tower walls to touch her. It wasn't their genitals that made her hurry to the window to hang up her hair. It was the stories they wrote about her. Volumes and volumes dedicated to the mythical princess and her endless braid. She barely minded when the men cried for their lost sight. She was guilty of keeping several dozen thorns beneath her pillow for safe-keeping. A princess never knew when a suitor might get too zealous in his advances. She had to be prepared. She knew all the horror stories that the

Sleeping Beauty girl had suffered. Five dozen pregnancies and not one that she could remember. It was a problem. If the men kept coming and her uterus continued working, she would always be vulnerable. Sleeping Beauty was never awake long enough to arm herself with the cursed spindle. She pushed a baby out and immediately fell back asleep. All the better for her though. She never had to feel the nursing blisters on her nipples or listen to the babies' daddies' complaints about how she never had the energy to pleasure them anymore. Rapunzel did what she could. She filled her mattress with glass shards and made sure that the thorns were sharpened. One to the eye was all it took. Then he would walk around her bedroom, sobbing into his hands, until a wrong step pitched him out the window and into the thorn garden below. Let him wander his dusty roads with the wood splinters jutting out of his eyelids. Rapunzel could still see. She had a braid to keep herself company and a line of suitors wrapping around the tower's walls. They all wanted to meet her. All she had to do was sing and pull them up when they found their way.

When she was five years old and already had a braid that stretched at least a mile, Rapunzel practiced wrapping electrical cords around her throat. The ogre kept her dressed in a wedding gown. It was supposed to shame her into staying a virgin. All it did was make her hungrier for meat. Rapunzel would climb in and out of the window, pulling at pork loins and lamb chops, sobbing for thick cuts of steak. She didn't mean to fill her chastity belt with meat but she couldn't help but satisfy everything her stomach wanted. Often, when a suitor asked to touch her golden hair, she would demand a basket of raw meat. Before and after sex, she would stuff the muscles in her mouth and sigh over the blood taste. She needed copper in her diet. When she couldn't have meat, she ate pennies until every swallow caused her stomach to clink. Repeatedly, the men tried guiding her to the bed but she just pushed them out the window. [Goodbye,] she sang in the voice men were supposed to die over. She laughed while they fell, cartwheeling in slow motion to the ground. The ogre would spend the night picking the men's meat off the thorn bushes. The resulting stew was Rapunzel's main meal come morning. She could taste a bit of herself in the broth. The problem with her body was simple: she impregnated men and they could not get used to the role change. Once inside her, she filled them with her egg. The resulting pregnancy scalded their abdomens as her egg took hold, until their belly flesh peeled off. She used to eat the dried pieces straight from their burning torsos until the ogre cracked her back in half. Then, every swallow was like another touch of the whip.

Rapunzel always found herself stuck between the ocean and a thorn forest. The suitors were in both places. Drowned or blinded. She never comforted their bloated and scarred bodies. What was the point? They would either forgive her or shave her bald. Rapunzel stood on a cliff and closed her eyes. She weaved thorns between her lashes and blinked rapidly until small holes appeared in the skin around her eyes. The suitors climbed briers and escarpments to reach her. She sniffed her armpits. There had to be a smell to her that made them so hungry, but she couldn't smell it. The ogre brought her blue and beige pieces of glass from the seashore. The water worn relics burned Rapunzel's hands. She milked the wounds into a chalice of sediment heavy wine. The ogre placed the glass on the windowsill. They heard the soft clacking of heels on stone. The dehydrating suitors, drawn to the musky scent of the wine, inevitably reached up and grabbed the glass. They drank deeply. Wine ran down the sweaty faces. They fell down. Rapunzel plugged her ears up with used condoms to mute the sound of flesh hitting ground. The ogre gnashed her teeth. [I am hungry,] the ogre said and Rapunzel fed her a handful of rotten parsley. They would have the bashed bodies for supper later that week, once the salted meat festered.

Rapunzel knew how to leave the tower. She wound her hair around a hook and lowered it halfway. When she jumped, her hair gently brought her to a stop just before her ankles would have smashed. She was able to touch the ground without her hair unraveling. She could walk for miles without her hair ever snaking off the claw.

To get back to her bedroom, she scaled the braid or flew a balloon if she could find one. She preferred to make her balloons out of her suitors' empty stomachs. The flesh kept the air confined and fresh. If she was lucky she would even have a couple. With her lovers' balloons overhead, Rapunzel could fly over the tower walls and past the thorn-filled ivy. The ogre never knew that the girl's footprints were embedded in the dirt around the outside of the tower. She couldn't imagine how Rapunzel escaped and returned undetected. From time to time, Rapunzel lacked the desire to help the suitors up the tower walls. She threw down the deflated balloons from her own travels. [Just blow it up. You'll be able to fly into my arms,] she called and laughed when they put their lips to the puckered ends of the preceding suitors. Fully inflated, the balloons rose, pulling the men with them. Suitors swallowed their swords to keep the balloons from popping. They frantically swung their feet to guide the balloons away from the thorns. Rapunzel waited until the top of the balloon was even with the window. She stuck a thorn into the fleshy globe while simultaneously pulling flesh from the stiff shoulders hanging below. Delighted Rapunzel screamed with the men as they fell in terror. The mirror chimed in. [Eeeeee, Ooooooo,] it rang cheerily, not understanding that the blood splashing onto its polished silver frame was from a fresh cut of shoulder. [Aaaaa,] Rapunzel said, guiding the glass in a three step waltz, the one the prince had taught her. The ogre carried the fallen men up Rapunzel's hair in a large woven wicker basket. The mirror opened its mouth. It wanted to be served first. It always wanted to be served first.

Once a month, Rapunzel ate a jeweled lime out of the ogre's mouth. The flesh was bitter and the skin tough but Rapunzel chewed it up like veal. Her stomach swelled from the juices. Seeds caught in her teeth. The suitors smelled her from miles away and ran into the tower sides to get closer. The ogre flossed with the mirror. [Do you know the little secret things about the art of seduction,] the ogre asked and Rapunzel nodded while halving the lime. She peeled the gemstones off the fruit and stuck them on the fronts of her teeth. She smiled prettily for the suitors clinging to the tower's stone face. [Did you miss me,] she asked and bit their fingers. The ogre pulled them up and swallowed them whole. Right down the gullet. The ogre pulled the bodies up and spoon-fed the softened flesh to Rapunzel. The mirror bounced on the wall. [I want some,] it shouted. [I want some! Pretty please?] It could eat five men whole and still feel hungry. [You stupid thing,] Rapunzel said. [You are always hungry. I can never satisfy you no matter how many men I feed you.] The mirror threw glass shards at her face. The pieces caught the flesh around her nose and eyes. She bled thickly. The blood smelled like warm summer tar. The ogre used the blood to caulk up the spaces in the bricks around the windowsill. [It will be winter soon,] she said. [This is no time to be idle, we have to prepare.] They used the men's hair to make fur coats. The tower had no heating system and in the winter even the milk froze. They bulked up with as much fat as they could stick onto their frames and sat huddled beneath the bed until the frost melted. In the meantime, the ogre fashioned Rapunzel a new vaginal plug to help keep her heat in. She slept for the three cold months and had to stay warm inside to be prepared for the onslaught of hungry men.

Just after the mother abandoned her in a parsley garden of the ogre to find, Rapunzel was diagnosed with lice. The tiny crab-like creatures traveled ten miles on the ass of a mule just to embed themselves in her scalp. She tore her nails off from all the itching. Her dress was in tatters. The ogre took a straight razor and ran the blade over Rapunzel's head. Her hair filled the tower. It took days for Rapunzel to remember how to breathe again. The breaths came strangely: in fits and bursts that tasted of vinegar and lemon. The ogre waved herbs beneath Rapunzel's nose and kissed her forehead. The lice fell out of her skin and dusted the floor. [I will eat them,] the glass announced and licked the parasites up while the young men screamed at the tower's base. [Where is the girl,] they shouted. The ogre screamed back, [She is far too young! And bald!] The men did not leave. They smelled her. Rapunzel rolled around on the floor, scratching at her head. She caught her right eye with the back of her thumb and went blind until the ogre could push in another jellied ball. The men's desirous shouting kept her up all night. The ogre fed her from a burned plastic bottle but Rapunzel did not close her eyes to sleep until the ogre pushed her blistered breast into the young girl's mouth. Her eyes swam around her face. The ogre spun gold from her belly button and fastened it to Rapunzel's head. The golden ribbon coiled on the ground. Glue dripped into Rapunzel's mouth. She sucked at the adhesive droplets. Her gums stuck together. The ogre pried them apart with a twisted stick of thorns. Rapunzel grabbed at the wood and suckled. Her mouth bled and she smiled.

Rapunzel carried her tower to the seashore and set it up on the rock face. The ogre sat bundled in her braid, protected by a ten foot barrier of hair. [I smell salt,] the ogre said, itching. A rash spread over her face. Rapunzel painted the ogre's face until she was featureless. [I feel unassuming,] the ogre said and shivered as she looked towards the sea. Drowned suitors rose from the waves. White foam covered them. With every step, they dissolved into thousands of droplets. Rapunzel opened her mouth and tasted them in the air. The salt air, musky with her suitors stink, aggravated her appetite. She ate shells and coarse sand. Her roots were growing out.

She was growing into a woman. Coal tinged her flaxen hair. The ogre dug a hole into the cliff and wriggled inside. She grabbed handfuls of sand worms and shoved them down Rapunzel's throat. [You never eat as much as you should,] she said while Rapunzel choked away her tears. Sand got inside her chastity belt. Rapunzel dug her hands inside to scratch the chaffed skin. The suitors reacted to the chastity belt's clang like they did a dinner bell. Rapunzel's skin came off in grated pieces. She collected the long curls of skin in her hands. Some of the skin caught in her hair. The ogre opened her mouth and ate the falling flesh. [Will we collect the men soon,] the ogre asked and Rapunzel grasped the more lecherous suitors by their throats. She squeezed until the spines snapped. [I am hungry for you,] Rapunzel said and pulled the flesh from their bones. The ogre crunched the bones and pushed the marrow out with her tongue. The congealed fat splashed into her eyes and the ogre worked her tongue around the sockets. [It is very good,] she said and Rapunzel clamored away from the beach, heading up the tower and into her bedroom. Everything was coated in salt grains. She brushed the tiny glass crystals off her mattress and lay down. The air dried over her. She was salted and left to cure. [Where is my savory herb rub?] Rapunzel asked but the suitors were not close enough to hear her and so there were no answers.

Rapunzel wielded a knife forged from three metals.

The tip was hardened platinum, the blade's body was folded steel, and the handle was cast iron. She licked along the serrated edge and tore her tongue open. She sat in the window and let the suitors practice climbing up her braid. She slashed their throats with the knife. The ogre sat in the thorns. She held up her basket and caught the men as they fell. [Will we eat them tonight,] the ogre asked. [I will,] the mirror said and broke its frame in half. Rapunzel looked into the halves and smiled at the solid tan of her face. She lifted the knife and slashed at her wrists. She touched the metals of her blade to her skin and bled. There was no need for sawing and grunting. [This is a sacrament, this is my blood,] she said and the suitors lifted their heads for a sip. She placed the scabs from her scalp on their tongues. [This is my body,] she said. The ogre poured green juice into the men's mouths. The men grew ovaries and a dry uterus. Their wombs contracted and bled. [Have some parsley,] the ogre said and served them bunches of fresh herbs. The men ate the parsley with their eyes closed. The fever lifted. Their fallopian tubes twisted and snaked out of their bodies through their anuses. The ogre wrenched the tubes free. [This is what parsley does,] she said and collected the appendages in her basket. She added several bouquets of fresh daisies while Rapunzel speared her eyes with the knife. The mirror helped push thorns into the jagged holes. [Oh my beauty,] the ogre sighed. [You are just so lovely.] Rapunzel placed the knife into her heart and pulled the organ out. [They can fight for it,] she said and tossed it down for her vaguely feminine suitors to fight over.

In the room farthest away from her bedroom, Rapunzel sank down on a floor covered with ribbons and lace. There was a cake in the center of the room, her name written across the top tier in chocolate frosting. Rapunzel peeled stained glass out of the icing and licked along the sides. She rested the cake beneath her arms. The suitors dove into the room with her. Rapunzel smeared each of their faces with cake. The icing clogged their throats. They clawed desperately at the ribbons on the floor as they drowned under the icing. They died smelling of lemon curd. The ogre crawled along the tiles and slid her way past the spun sugar fabric. [Don't I mean anything,] she asked as Rapunzel shoved gallons of pureed parsley down the ogre's throat and watched her turn inside out. [I will miss you, Mother,] Rapunzel sighed as she pulled the dead womb free from her gasping monster. She swallowed it whole and let the ogre sink down beautifully into the tulle and silk. [I will remember you,] she promised. Rapunzel stabbed a finger with a needle and waited for a bead of blood to well up. She flicked the droplet towards the departing ogre and sighed deeply. [Now who will protect me from the suitors,] she asked. The doors opened and the men barged in. Fabric tangled around their ankles, yanking them down. Rapunzel leaned forward and opened her mouth wide. The men went down her throat and drowned in her stomach acid. They kicked her insides like tiny babies. Repeatedly she struck her abdomen with a fist until they quieted. When they stopped kicking, she rested one hand against her stomach and pressed her other hand against Sleeping Beauty's spindle. The spindle was her plan B. She was so tired. The curse did its job. She finally rested, albeit for 3,000 years. The cake remained moist, the icing delicious.

Little Red Twisted Hood – Act Two

She killed the wolf out of obligation. The grandmother and huntsman stared. Each had a knife and a net. So Red sliced through the wolf's gut and closed her eyes when his bowels fell out. His fur had a sickly sweet smell. Like lemonade mixed with meat, glazed with smoke and raw sugar. She'd rather the beast die by her hand than a stranger's. The grandmother would let each cut linger until he fell apart in the midst of a yawn. The huntsman would hammer the wolf to the ground, then practice sharpening his blades while the wolf grunted and strained to get up from the floor. Not Red. She sliced fast, moving her arm up and down in one motion, severing the ligaments and opening the body. It was all so the wolf wouldn't suffer. She could barely stand the sight of his eyes glazing over in pain. They had fallen in love outside a meat shop, when she went to buy a pound of ground chuck and he was waiting for a cut of chicken breast. They ate rolled

roast beef in a stranger's basement, then stuck their hands into each other's hair. She hadn't had her basket then. He had given it to her as a gift, weeks later, when she said she would visit the grandmother's house. Familial obligation and all that. But the grandmother had studied the wicker and questioned the tell-tale scratch marks on the handle. [Kill him or we'll do it for you,] she said. [It's not like you should be surprised. You knew this was the risk when you went to him,] the grandmother reminded Red and pulled her old hunter lover out of the closet where he had been hiding. So Red found a long-bladed knife in the kitchen drawer and invited the wolf to lunch. She let him get to dessert, his favorite meal, before she severed his navel.

Red found the blue house and paused before entering. It was one thing for a hunter to have an ax but another for a man to simply carry the blade on his shoulder. The door opened and Red went inside. [I am the red maiden,] she said and the master pointed to her room. [Sit in silence for an hour,] he said from where he sat on the ground. His feet were pointed inward so that his toes pressed together. He shuffled when he stood to walk. Red felt for the tiny dagger she kept in her basket. It was meant for lupine rapists but ax-wielding grooms were just as dangerous. The man went into the room and gave her an egg. [Go into my secret room,] he whispered as he shuffled out. Red put the egg in her basket. She wrapped tissue paper around it. She slid the basket beneath the bed. [Once upon a time, a girl went into a forest and was accosted by a guillotine. It took her head but she wasn't willing to go around without her neck. She bent the blade of the guillotine and snapped the wood of its frame. That was it. Her spinal column grew back and the wolf sat alone in a corner, crying,] the man explained from beyond the doorway. Undeterred Red went down into the basement. She swung open the unlocked secret door and sat in the puddles of blood. There were skinned wolf carcasses everywhere, heads still attached but without the fur. Red dragged the bodies up into her bedroom, laid them in a pile, and sat on top. She ate the egg the man had given her and spit chewed up yolk over the wolves' pointed faces. Their snouts moistened and their eyelids blinked. The jaws creaked while parting. She sewed up the stomach gaps as best she could. The man came home and the furless wolves crouched down on their hunches. They were ready to eat his beard.

Guilty, Red punctured herself in the back and let the blood stain spread over her white cape and hood. Because her blood turned brown too quickly, Red splashed herself with scarlet dye and let the color soak in. The colors and the guilt of her complicity weighed Red down. The only thing she could think of was red—blood red, crimson blood red. Red clouds and red trees and red furless wolves, panting in the forest while pulling their red genitals apart with red hand-like paws. She was red. Red. Little Red. Small Red. She was one of them. The reddest of them all. Grandmother would have been panicked by the intensity of her hue. Red vibrated with her color. She hummed. The witch who watched her from afar broke her mirror as the red spread across the panes. Red dropped onto the floor and let the blood collect in her basket. She added gelatin and stirred the mixture with a stick until the blood congealed. She ate scoops of blood jelly with a steel spoon. The iron in the blood mixed with her copper saliva. Her mouth was a metalworker. It hissed molten steel. Red went to each wolf she found in the man's house. She stuck them with a pitchfork and tapped into their heaving sides. Red siphoned gallons of blood through a cheesecloth filter and boiled the fluid down until it was a salty syrup. She baked a sponge cake and poured the blood honey over the batter. The wolves roaming the forest smelled the cake covered in their kin's blood and honey. They scratched at the front door. She threw cake slices up the fireplace and listened as they leaped onto the roof, snatching at the pieces of cake flying past. Some wolves weren't so lucky and fell over the eaves. Others tumbled down the chimney. The ones who fell down the chimney were drained for a blood wine. Red seasoned each glass with a prick of her finger. Eighteen ceilings were stamped with her crimson silhouette for the eighteen wolves that died for her blood honey cake. It was not something that she was proud of, but it was part of the deal.

In penance, Red shaved her scalp bald. The exposed muscle and bone turned a bright red color that shined brightly in the forest. Red giggled when the wolves tried licking her brains out. They picked up pieces of her cerebellum with the tips of their tongues. Everything Red touched turned bright red. At night, she suffered from terrible diarrhea and lay out under the moon on the grass. All the feces were a deep crimson color. She bled out several times a day but always managed to survive by sucking a mandrake dry. The roots' milk was so full of protein that by the next hour, Red was back on her feet and chopping through the forest. When not bleeding, Red cut into her wrists and drained the wounds into a plastic bucket. The wolves stood far away, weary of her fecal blood's scent. She planned on removing her fingers by the next full moon but got distracted by the fat her grandmother kept in chafing dishes arranged on the dining room table. Red ate her butter and lard, her shortening and oils. She ate until her veins clogged and the arteries pulsed red on her scalp. The wolves worked a razor around the top of her skull, shaving the scarlet layer by layer. They placed every slice on the backs of their tongues and let the skin melt onto their taste buds. Red peeled layers off her eyeballs and fed the wolves gel. Red went to the mirror and stared at the glass. She sewed a red hat onto her head and worked the silk around the sides of her face. She was a little red hood girl and didn't need any hair to hide that.

Red smelled death. The stench sat in her basket and turned into liquid. Red put her arm inside and fished out handfuls of the liquid. She drank slowly and the saccharine fluid coated her tongue. Each time she swallowed her saliva, it was like taking another sip. The stench attracted the wolves. Red walked quickly, the fluid sloshing over the sides of the basket, wetting the ground, and forming a path to the grandmother's house. The wolves walked with their noses to the ground. They breathed heavily. Their mouths stayed close to the backs of her shoes. From time to time, they nipped her and Red stumbled. Her grandmother's house stunk the worst. She kept the smell in her oven. Rotten meat collected in her walls, piling up against the ceiling and forcing the floorboards to sag. The grandmother went around with a napkin pressed to her face to block out the odor. She ate sugar cubes. Black mold covered her fingernails. Red pulled the house boards back and slipped into the crawlspace over the foundation. The wolves pawed at the planks to pull her out. They got stuck in the eaves while trying to climb in through the chimney. Red picked at her grandmother's rotten meat piled under her house. Her engorged stomach wouldn't fit fully through the spaces in the kitchen walls. Grandmother called the girl up, brought a knife from the kitchen and carved the girl's gut. [Thank you, grandmother,] Red said and skipped away. Green water filled the sinks. Red drank what she could stomach and left the rest outside for the wolves. They vomited between sips. The smell made them hunger for meat but as soon as they ate, their starving bowels emptied.

Red was a killer. She never went anywhere without a picnic basket filled with sharp blades. She carried swords and knives, razor blades and scissors. She kept each edge razor sharp. Red knocked down her grandmother's house and dug a hole through the foundation. She poured concrete to form a thick slab along the ground and waited for the trees to push up against the slab. Limestone dripped and formed stone knives that draped along the walls. Red lured the wolves inside. She sacrificed every wolf she came upon. One knife worked around the bottom of the chin while another sliced across the shoulder blades, coming up the back of the neck. Red yanked the spines out. She skinned the bodies and left the pelts on the forest paths. They served as mile markers, strung up in the trees. Red sat with the wolves as they rotted. When the meat softened, Red smeared the bones across the walls. The tree trunks jabbed the bodies' sides. The stone knives skewered them. The bones stuck to the limestone, becoming calcified rock. Red climbed out of the concrete hole she had built and walked through the forest. She moved her hood aside and flashed her legs at the wandering men. The hunters followed her. They wielded their axes and panted, breaths hot with desire. Little Red brought them back to the hole ringed with wolf bones and flayed them. She fed their muscles to the few still-breathing canines. The wolves howled. They chewed the axes and opened their stomachs from the inside. Red stripped naked and painted her genitals bright red. She let the dye dry and sat with the dead. They all, man and wolf, worshiped her red hood. As she knew they would.

Little Red Hood wasn't just one girl. She was the Sleeping Beauty and the Snow White girl. She was the ill-fated stepdaughter and the beast's slave. Little Red Hood was simply the girl who donned the red hood and ran away from everything. She ran from the witches, the needles and the spindles, from the poison apples, the pomegranates and the roses. She exchanged her past for hungry wolves. The wolves waited patiently for Little Red Hood to approach. They sat in a faux grandmother's house, wearing an old woman's night-gown and slippers, each in their own bed. They chewed on old meat pieces and tapped their claws against the walls, impatient for the girl to knock on the door. She rapped on the wall twice and the wolves let her in. She sat at the dining room table. The house was warm but stuffy from all the wolves pretending to sleep. Little Red Hood sneezed from the dander floating in the air. Her skin itched. She ate all the dishes the wolves offered her. Roasted loin with a dry pepper rub and blood honey cake. Her stomach heaved as she swallowed. She bit and chewed, tore and choked the slices down. Then the wolves went beneath her skirt. They parted her thighs. They all did things to her body together. Little Red Hood gasped and clawed at the table. She had no need for fruits or glass caskets. She didn't need a ball gown or a prince to rescue her from the basement torture chamber. She just needed the wolves' manes between her fingers so she could tug on the fur and keep their heads in the right position. They weren't even dogs. They were simply hairy men. They had always only been hairy men. She knew this all along. Red didn't mind that the wolves refused to shave their faces. She liked their hair against her legs. She forgot life in the other kingdoms and orgasmed with each bite of the proffered loin.

Red burned herself in a fire. She stuck her head into a volcano and walked over the dried lava streams. Magma churned and Red's eyes burned from the sulfur smell. She choked but pulled her hood tighter. She trotted quickly, her heels digging into the stones. Her skin broke. Red was prepared for tectonic plate shifts and hellfire. She ate the lava burning through her ankles. She fed the wolves to the fire. They winced and turned bright red. She waited until they were cooked to medium well, then pulled them out by their tails. Each piece of meat was chased with a sprinkle of crushed stone. Undaunted, Red swam through the lava. She came out the other end and struggled onto the purgatory hills. The wolves growled and snapped at her legs. She kicked them away. Bipedal wolves standing on their hind legs hit her with whips and pitchforks. They stabbed her in the spine. Red crawled on her knees under their savagery. The wolves threw knives at her. She grabbed the blades for herself and stabbed at them wildly, blinded by the sulfur. She cut herself instead. She gutted her stomach. Paper bags and her grandmother fell out. Red vomited liquid magma. There were raw, undigested wolf heads caught in her intestinal tract and she pushed hard to get them out. The struggles caused her stomach to split further, the seam ripping her almost in half. She kicked the heads out of her and fell onto the ax she had stolen from the hunter. It broke her back. The hunter came out of her spinal cord, followed by her faceless mother, who crawled through the bloody muck with a mourning veil draped over her head. The hunter grabbed Red by the neck. She saw her reflection in his eyes and recognized in him the wolf head she had eaten. The man peeled her meat, cutting off the rest of her hood. He left her naked and helpless in the volcano pit.

Rapunzel's Parsley – Act Three

Midsummer. Beyond the wall is a garden. The mother looks out her bedroom window and hungers. Her tongue is always swollen, the tip furred and tingling. Baskets of rotted fruit line the bedroom walls. She steps over half-eaten bananas and smashed oranges. The walled garden is not hers. She has never seen anyone tend the wild vines heavy with fruits. The harvest beckons to her. In the center of this secret garden are fragrant bushes of parsley. She is pregnant. Her belly is heavy and swollen. She is tired of being pregnant. The mother scales many walls because of her hunger. She devours three kings, then five dozen of their armed men. And still she tells herself that she is famished. The mother takes a running start over the wall and hurls herself into the garden. The weeds slap at her belly as she rolls along the ground like a giant potato bug. Thorns prick her skin. She falls onto her stomach many times. There is no need for her hands to

fly out. Let the swollen womb break her fall. The mother thinks of her closet and the many rows of iron hangers, each one full of promise. She stands and waddles to the parsley bushes. There, delighted by the smell, she shoves her face into the plants' centers. Parsley sticks between her teeth. Parsley shoves itself up her nose. Parsley sticks out her ears. The mother is simply a sack of almost maternal parsley. She laughs as the herbs twist and grind between her teeth. She has never tasted anything so green. The juice has a piquant flavor. A bit of bitterness. A minty sweetness. She chews while hammering on her stomach. [Get out,] she hisses between clenched teeth. The unborn child kicks back. It signals the witch. [I want more parsley,] the mother howls as the hag approaches. [You are tired of the child,] the old woman asks. The mother slaps the old woman's shoulders. [You can have her if I can just have another parsley plant,] she says. [Agreed,] the old woman says, holding up a mesh sieve. Between blinks she reaches between the mother's thighs and scoops the child free. The placenta drops off the child's body and lands on the ground. There it sprouts. Sweet minty green parsley shoots up from the uterine tissue on the ground. Grinning the mother touches her svelte stomach. She falls to her knees and eats the newly grown bush. The fetal child coos in the old woman's hands. The mother's fallopian tubes snake out of her body. They are brown intestines of fertility. [Take it all,] the mother says. [Only leave me with the parsley.] The reproductive organs fall out as she eats fistfuls of the herb. Her organs lie scattered around her. The hag places the child to her sagging breast. [Feed now,] the hag says to the child and it burrows in through the nipple. The hag winces and grimaces as the baby suckles greedily.

Parsley covered Rapunzel. The witch macerated the herbs with some rum and sugar, then smeared the girl's body with the paste. Rapunzel's skin was green. She felt her tubes dying. Everything shriveled slowly. Her ovaries shed their eggs, one at a time, tiny sacs wilted from dehydration. The eggs collected at the base of her uterus. She shook her hips and her ovaries rattled like the tail of a rattlesnake. Her organs turned into dried hot peppers. She imagined cutting her pelvis open like a cap and shaking the eggs out onto a clean white dish. Those millions of eggs would make a thin coat across the plate. They would look like salt crystals. Maybe she would count them, her tiny dried egg babies. Every day, the witch bathed Rapunzel in hot water steeped with parsley leaves. Her skin dried out completely. Her hands greened. Her nails were a sickly gangrenous yellow. The witch plaited Rapunzel's long hair with parsley stems. The smell covered her sourness. She leaned out the tower window and vomited. She threw up whole parsley leaves, then entire bushes. Instead of dangerous thorny vines, parsley surrounded the tower. Anyone who tried rescuing her would be rendered infertile. Rapunzel imagined squeezing out one single infant, its face screwed up and red. It would wail. The child would be a simple torso and a head. She was sure that it would be a human sea monkey. She might nurse it for a night or two before the limbless creature flopped out of her embrace to the tower window. It would teeter on the sill. She imagined it falling many stories before being impaled by the same parsley bushes that destroyed its prenatal state. Still, perhaps to fulfill her dreams, Rapunzel took handfuls of parsley with each meal. At night, she slept with three parsley leaves under her pillow in the hopes she could divine her future husband's face.

Rapunzel leaped from her tower. No prince waited at the bottom to catch her. She simply threw herself. The Jump of Faith. The Leap of Divine Inspiration. She kept her eyes closed. Rapunzel fell for many years. She aged. Her blond hair developed silver streaks. She landed on a giant mushroom cap and whimpered. The fungus was more potent than the parsley she had grown up with. She sniffed the mushroom cap and bit its flesh. It tasted bitter. She foamed at the mouth and spat on the ground. A giant tree grew from the bubbling liquid. The fruits had top hats and wrinkled baby faces. [Mama,] they shrieked at her. Rapunzel ran into a red river. Humanoid carp swam around her. They nibbled her feet. Several tried humping her ankles. Rapunzel stripped off her dress and donned a blue squash growing on the banks. The gourd came down to her knees. She hiked it up with a hand-shaped vine slung over her shoulders. [May I have your children,] a man dressed as an elephant asked. Rapunzel bit her tongue and showed him the parsley leaves sprouting from her groin. The man touched the leaves and winced. His pants dropped. His genitals grew legs and skipped away. [I have lost my manliness,] the man gasped and started after his escaping member. Gourded, Rapunzel traveled on. A queen dressed in bright green stepped into her path. [I would like to trade wombs,] the queen said. She pointed to the many children sprouting out of the ground behind her. [Give me your infertility and I will give you a working system.] Shrieking in disgust, Rapunzel kicked the children's stems and jumped onto a toadstool. [Infertility did not come easily to me. Now I only trust the mushrooms,] Rapunzel replied. The queen screamed, outraged at the disobedience. Crouched on the fleshy cap, Rapunzel turned inside out. Her womb covered her wholly. She felt safe inside the reproductive bladder. Noise was muted. Amniotic fluid filled her nostrils. She grew plugs over her most vulnerable orifices. Rapunzel settled inside of herself. There was just enough room for her to move comfortably. She did not even notice the jackals kicking her parsley-infested uterus down the street, dried eggs rattling inside the womb bag like rocks.

The prince tried to save her but failed. Parsley bushes

grew through his eyes as he climbed out of the garden and up her tower. He came near the top and dropped back down, the vines pulling his penis off and casting it into the now shark-infested moat. Laughing joyously Rapunzel emasculated him as he fell. She took her morning toast and parsley jam and smeared the bread across her face. The parsley juice sunk into her eyes. The irises turned bright green. The whites became green. Soon, all of her face was a verdant color. Rapunzel blinked several times. Behind her lids, everything was washed over with a green hue. She opened her eyes and saw that the green filter had spread. She took a running start for the window. It was a brighter green than the many objects scattered about the room. She tossed herself over the ledge and fell. The parsley grabbed at her womb and tried to pull it out. She bounced several times at the bottom. Her eyes burned. She cried solid salt flakes. Determined and penis-less, the prince called to her, parsley needles sticking out of his eyelids. They touched their blindness together, his of the shadowed variety and hers of hay. When they kissed, the parsley came up from her stomach and punished him where his penis used to be.

The man demanded, [Give me your alfalfa sprout, your bean sprouts, and those beet greens you keep hidden beneath your shirt.] He said, [I am in love with your blue green eyes, with your bluish-green skin, and with that bottle green fuzz between your legs. It is a lush lettuce garden of delight. Don't you remember that there were chard mushrooms where we went and the skies were a lush chartreuse, although the men who lived there said that it was simply chop-suey green poison? Some plants give off common sorrel gases that can make everyone sick. Too many dandelion greens can poison an expecting mother's baby, did you know that?] Oh, then the man said, [I love your emerald throat, the way that French sorrel above your collar bone moves when you speak, and your greenishness when you strip your clothes away revealing that inner jade you keep so well concealed. My leaf beet, my olive green, my Paris green and pea green, how I wish I could have pigweeds with you, beautiful sage green salad greens and twin sea greens. Oh my spinach beauty, I cannot live without touching your stemmed beet. Let me masticate those sprouts you keep so private. Let me possess your Swiss chard and make you my teal wife, my very own turnip green. You are the brightest and cleanest of all the village greens; there is no one who has wild celery such as yours, you yellow-green mistress, you keeper of the Viridity Tower and parsley kale grounds.] Though I heard none of it, this he said and more.

There was a prince born with female reproductive organs instead of male. From childhood, he was in a constant state of pregnancy although there was no child within him. He craved the sea lettuce that an infirm witch spent a lifetime growing at the edge of her favorite pond.

For many days and nights, he dreamed of this fragrant lettuce, of pulling the leaves apart and biting into their crispness. The witch tended to her lettuce by the moonlight. She weeded and washed her harvest with loving, careful devotion. Head by head, the witch took the lettuce to her ward, which she kept trapped in a tower. One time, the prince sneaked after her and stole one of the leaves she had just harvested as it lay drying in the moonlight. Still, the prince was not satisfied by the single leaf he ate. He wanted a whole bunch of leaves, so he followed the witch to the tower and watched as she cleared her throat and a thick braid of hair fell from the sky. The witch tugged the hair three times and floated up the walls. After she came back down and ran away, the prince cleared his throat and stood at the tower's base. The braid fell. He tugged it three times and rose up. He followed the braid into the tower. There, he saw a princess on a bed. Her back was to him. [I am so hungry for your sea lettuce,] the prince said as his womb drummed within. The girl turned. He stared at the enormous head of sea lettuce and the spread of leaves that nearly made a face. The girl made a muffled sound. She reached down his throat and stole the single sea leaf from his stomach. He gagged on her arm as she extracted the leaf and ate it. The leaves of her face moved and crunched as she ate. The leaves spread enough for him to see the stem sticking up from her torso. The masculinity of the girl's stem taunted him.

Unable to control himself, the prince fell upon the girl and tried to eat her face. She bit him. Her leaves turned bright red. They shuddered and fanned out. She swallowed him whole and sighed. The witch returned with an ax so the girl could cut away at the unfortunate vegetation that grew so plentifully from within her abdomen.

A Rapunzel princess, one of many, sat in a tower behind three stories of lace veils. Because she had lived off of parsley bushes for the entirety of her youth, she lacked vocal cords and a womb. Filled with parsley, the girl was rarely hungry. In those instances that a young man vaulted into her tower, the girl extended her arms and caught him. [You are so lovely,] the boy always said. The Rapunzel princess would smile and gently touch his neck while her womb screamed. She would scrape flesh from bone and throw the enamel pieces of his teeth beneath her bed. She did not mind this cannibalistic infertility. The young men's belief that she was so innocent and so vulnerable while trapped in the tower amused her. She could leave if she chose to. She had scissors to cut the veils and a rope ladder that touched the ground. But Rapunzel enjoyed her silent room and the way she forced her visitors to be mute within her. For once she ate them, they rarely said a word.

Rapunzel tired of her tower and hair. She shaved it off and put on a short black wig. She placed a mirror with her picture embedded in the glass within the witch's bedroom chambers. Rapunzel giggled as the witch scratched and clawed at the glass. [I must be beautiful,] the witch screamed and threw her ax at the princess. Unperturbed, the princess stuffed an apple down her throat and fell into the local bar while gagging. Someone, thinking she meant disrespect when she bumped into them, shoved her head into a glass mug of barley wine. The only prince there shattered the glass against the bar top and gathered her up lovingly in a Heimlich maneuver. But that was not enough to dull the pain. Rapunzel decided that a spinning wheel would put her to sleep. She had heard stories about the magic of spindles, and so she ran up the tower steps and pulled a spindle out from beneath her bed. Her eyes widened and her mouth dropped in a look of feigned surprise. She threw her hair, now long again, out the window and stroked the mandrel. A wood splinter caught her finger and stuck. She staggered around the room and fell onto her bed. Her hair tugged from outside. She heard footsteps outside the tower. A man came up her braid and turned her over, dazed as she was. She tried not to whimper as he kissed and groped her. With what little energy she had, she lifted her arms to resist his affections. Dejected, he jumped out the window again and she woke up. She heard hoof-beats. [I will be in love with a beast then,] she sighed and threw herself from the window. She turned around and around, pirouetting before landing on a briar patch. She fastened her hair around her like a hooded cloak. A man-beast strode towards her. He picked her up with one hand. [Let me restore your humanity,] she said as she ate a wilting rose. She plunged a branch of parsley into the lovesick beast's chest. Turning, she walked away, wooden needles sticking out of the soles of her feet. [I am done,] she sighed. [There is nothing more human than that] and she left the bleeding beast for the wolves.

Rapunzel drank too much parsley wine and fell out the tower window. With broken legs, she stumbled through the witch's garden, pulling up herbs and flowers with her toes. Men ran after her, clawing at her clothing and hair. She batted them away with her claws. Rapunzel found a parsley bush and bunched the leaves up. She shoved them deep inside her body through both of her lowly holes. This gave her an herb stuffed womb. Her inner self blistered. Her thigh flesh was raw. Rapunzel broke alcoholic gourds and drank the contents. She watered her fallopian tubes and waited for the spoiled eggs to crack. When the herbs were nearly matured, she bent over backwards. The parsley sprouted from her body. It came out of her vagina, anus, and navel. Rapunzel laughed; never had her parsley been so plentiful. Virgin girls, wanting to keep their purity, came to her and ate her leaves. Rapunzel gathered their discarded wombs in a thorny bag. She hid them in the bush's roots between her legs.

Though people said otherwise, Rapunzel could not

sing. She could not let go of her hair in great tumbling braids from her tower window. She could not shave the locks that enslaved her. Instead she ate everything the witch offered. She drank the sour mother's milk from her withered breast and looked longing at the razor. She gazed at the parsley growing below. Everything she ate and drank tasted of parsley. She thought about princes and wondered if they would smell of parsley or have parsley eyes or parsley mouths or parsley genitals that would mutilate her reproductive organs when they should be fertilizing her. Rapunzel never forgot the witch's garden that she could see when peering out from between her mother's legs as a child, so close, yet so far away. She remembered how the parsley felt brushing against the inside of her womb. Rapunzel had parsley every day of her life. She slept with it. She bathed with it. She could not get the smell of it out of her nose. She wanted a prince to save her. She did not want the prince to go blind. She wanted him to fall in love with her blindly. She wanted him to fall in love with parsley. Rapunzel nearly died in infancy. She nearly died when in her mother—her mother who wanted parsley because she did not want Rapunzel. The witch grew the parsley and wanted Rapunzel. The witch did not want Rapunzel to have children. She did not want Rapunzel to grow and become a mother, but to stay the same. The witch had already stolen so many children from all the mothers who wanted her parsley. She had eaten those children. But Rapunzel was different. Rapunzel was the one who wasn't supposed to die, who didn't die. Rapunzel was the one born of parsley and meant to have nothing inside of her. The witch wanted her to be washed clean. The witch filled her with parsley as a warning. The witch told the boys to stay away or they would get thorns in their eyes. The witch wanted the parsley to grow thick and cover her only child, keeping her that way. The boys, crafty as they were, got in anyway. The boys did not know what parsley could do. The boys fell in love with the girl in the tower. The boys loved Rapunzel right there in her room in the tower. She loved them back. Rapunzel loved them all, then they all fell to the ground, tore their eyes on the thorns, and went blind. The blind boys tried to do what men should still be able to. Blind, the boys tried impregnating the princess. Rapunzel simply touched their unseeing eyes with her parsley-tinted fingertips and said, [No, no, I cannot have children. I am parsley and I cannot sprout.] The witch, who had made her this way, knew this but the boys did not. The boys tried to fill her belly with babies, but instead they went blind and had nothing. Rapunzel filled her eyes with parsley to stop her tears. She pretended that her body was a witch's garden and that her sad, hungry mother was coming back to eat her leafy greens. And so she waited.

PART TWO

MY
ESTROGEN

Lilith's Extra Rib – Act One

[Shall I be a Lilith woman?] I suffer from the ribbed cyst. So the Lilith woman tempts me. She brings me into the heat and leaves me to my burning fate. But this is better than what it once was. Once upon a time, a man thought he owned me and so he laid me across a bamboo cutting block and carved the rib from my chest. He cloned the bone and gave me back both pieces. This made it so that I had an extra piece of rib jutting from my breast. It was uncomfortable to walk and the jutting ribs made me think of barbecue sauce daily. That and pickled vegetables. [Let me sprout wings and see if the man can chain me down,] I said. I knew no angel that had wings like mine. I cut through stone and ice. I left the slivers for the man to find. He bleeds bright red so I know where to find him. But my blood is copper. I used to think it was blue. Someone told me about the azure veins and I believed them. They were wrong. The blood was a burnt

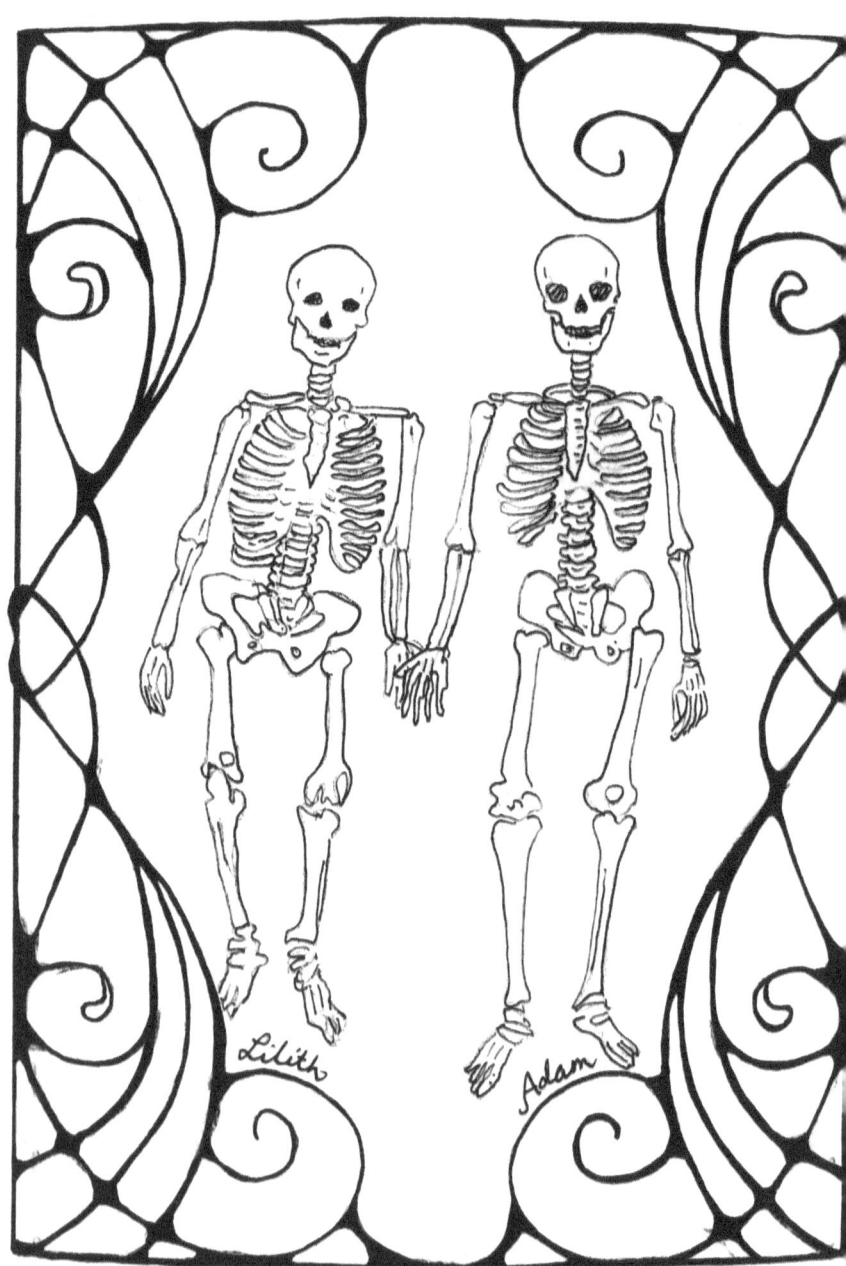

gold. Men came from the farthest reaches of the world to beg me for a droplet. I gave them nothing, not a flake nor a scab. If they want to reach immortality, they need to sacrifice a finger, or a toenail. [Straight into the cannibal moon's gaping mouth, I marveled.] I cover my eyes in mock horror. [Goodbye, extra digits. Meet my ribs and sire one another,] I said to him. While he fingered my rib, I took up an ax because the woman told me so. She said to cut him, so I did.

There are snake vines over me. They grow iron wings and slither across my thighs. [Shall you be a part of us,] they ask and I pull my face off. Beneath my chin is a mask. It is not like any other mask. [No, I do not carry the latex covering with me. I keep the plastic to myself. I hold onto the real flesh,] I tell the snakes. Hearing this the man crawls out of the garden and offers me his hand. [Shall I take those fingers,] he asks. They are slick with dirt. I stare at the nails and see worms wriggle up from the enamel bed. I push the man back. [You really should love me,] the man says. Shall I love the man? I wonder. Or should I let him go free? Let him wander through the desert until he reaches the ocean at the other end of this land. Lilith whispers in my ear. She says that I should give him a drink of water, then use him as a willing sacrifice. She says that his name belongs on the chamber doors, that his letters are etched across the bottom of the tree trunk. It was he who carved them there. [Adam, oh my Adam,] I sing, reading the letters slowly and I beat him with a branch from the very same tree. There were demons in the closets but now they sit on my bed with their heads in their hands. They watch me as I slide past. They give me apple slices. I dip each piece of the fruit into lemon butter. [I am hungry,] I say. [Eat the man,] they say. Lilith whispers into my ear, [The man will taste like roasted beef.] She gives me the knife. I chew what parts of him I can get my teeth through. He tastes more like raw veal than roasted beef.

If there is another woman I will chain her down. I will chain the Eve. Then I will chain Persephone. Then the other queens who strip their bones of meat and leave their marrow naked. I pity the calcium. It begs to be covered. I find Eve on the dining room table, legs open. [I am his wife now,] she says and points at the framed photograph of my Adam. [You are nothing but fermented meat,] I hiss at her. I eat Adam's image, glass and all. My tongue rips. My teeth crack. If I am not the one who denied the fruit, am I the one that plucked it? Was it even an apple? Or is it just a red fruit? A quince? Or a pomegranate? Some red bulbous food built around mortality. That is why Lilith stayed alive. She didn't burden herself with death. She let the husband and wife fight over the seeds and dig their own graves with the cores. [After you decapitate her, put her head into the refrigerator,] Lilith whispers as I place Eve's head into the freezer. She is an

Eve cube. The first wife Popsicle. A wifesicle. I let her thaw until she is soft and pudgy, then I freeze her again. Lilith claps her hands gleefully. She thinks the whole silly affair is a hoot. [There are men waiting for you,] she says and points at the walls. The plaster is lined with rows of holes filled with jutting genitals. Their mouths chew the paint. I drink a shot glass of liquid soap and foam covers my tongue. Lilith lays me down. She braids my hair into snake skins. With her eyes closed, she gives me a handful of teeth. [Plant them and they will become men,] she says. I do and they do.

[If I am not the first woman, I will not settle for the second,] I announce to anyone who will listen. I sit on the fruit branch of the apple tree and allow the Adam man to eat the fruit from between my legs. There was not a tree. There was never a tree. Instead, the truth is that the woman (I) spread her thighs and revealed the branches extending from her womb (mine). The man, Adam, pulled the fruits off my vines. They tasted like bitter strawberries. Their mouthfeel was like overly ripe cherries. His mouth turned bright red. There are many other bushes outside. In pretending to be the tree, I tuck the leaves inside of me. The man walks up to me on his knees. He licks my kneecaps. There are citrus fruits inside the bones. His teeth rot the longer he waits to gargle. Lilith gave the first man and the second woman a basket of the most delicious vegetation. There were foot carrots and hand limes and many genital grapes. Lilith urged them to eat. The woman pretended to devour a fingerling potato but let it drop past her lips instead. The first man and the second woman didn't eat and instead turned into bone. I turned into bone. Now I sit alone in the back of my closet and place my head in a garment bag crying. Lilith pulls the fabric out of my mouth. [You are meant to feed the wicked,] she says and offers me a silver platter of fruits. The fruits look like tiny severed heads. [You won't find any preachers here,] she says and kisses my shoulder. She peels one green fruit and reveals the black-speckled meat inside. The core reflects her face. She winks and grins and files her nails on her chin. [It is better than nothing,] she confides to me.

I raise fruits in the kitchen cabinets. When they ripen, they splatter me in the face. Their juice burns. It is too acidic. Then my thighs itch. I sit in the sink and Lilith washes me. She soaps my shoulders with baking soda and adds a layer of all-purpose flour. [We did not bake in the garden,] she says and I drink chocolate directly from a bottle. [There was no chocolate, either,] she says. She has told me stories about the garden before. She mentioned the enviable fruits and all the trees that were like living skyscrapers, each towering in the sky. The branches were made of glass. When Lilith glared, the glass shattered and cut the Adam man's upper lip. Then she smiled and all the glass grew again. [What if the trees had been mirrors?] I ask as Lilith eats a pineapple, thorns and all. [We had no need for mirrors,] she says. [We weren't supposed to know we were naked.] She shows me the spot under her ribs where her extra breast sprouted from. The breast is so small, I can barely see it. The mammary gland is more like a birth mark, a strange little mole. I poke the nipple and Lilith shivers with excitement. [You don't understand,] she says as she opens every door in the house. [I can't breathe when you do that,] she says as she lets the air in. She lets Adam in. He sits in a corner, crying. His eyes are bruised. We force his swollen lids open. There are fruit peels shoved into the gray sides of his cheeks. No wonder he is crying.

It isn't only a rib that Lilith has a spare of. She also has an extra eye, an extra teat, and a third leg. She milks both her teat and her extra leg in the kitchen sink. I collect the droplets. Her milk is thick and bright yellow. It is amber. Honey colored. Rotten. It is liquid cheese. It smells of chlorine. I drink a glass and vomit. Lilith paints her face bright red with her mixture of pigments and fats. She rubs her fists against the walls and leaves furrows in the plaster. [Was this how you left Eden?] I ask and Lilith shows me photographs of the forbidden tree. It is really a shrub. A tiny bush. With branches covered with thorns. Lilith's name is written across the roots. I take a razor blade to the photograph and scrape along the outer lines of the letters. [Once upon a time,] Lilith says. [I knew a man who thought he was more than just mud. We were born simultaneously, sprouted from the same dirt clot. But the man said he was metal and I was leaves. So he tried tearing me apart. I threw water in his face and he ran off like liquid. And that was the end of the garden. It flooded with his organs and I flew away before the fluid could touch me. Once upon a time, I found a hidden garden and climbed inside. The dirt was pale gray and dotted with brilliant red flowers. I plucked the petals and every bloom had a nectar head at the center. They oozed sweet honey.] Lilith digs the pollen out of the corners of her eyes and smears the yellow across the stove top. She pulls at the spinal cords from her neck.

[But I found a woman in her coffin,] Lilith explains. She digs her nails into her wrists and shifts her eyes upwards. [Were you in the garden, too?] I ask and Lilith sticks her hands into the dirt. [I should have known that the man would steal from me,] she says. She lifts the thin fabric covering her stomach to reveal the jagged scar covering her upper torso. [Deep inside there was a rib,] she says and parts the scar. She fishes around and hands me a tiny sliver of bone. Later, I plant this bone and wait outside for it to sprout. The tree that emerges from the marrow is a pale mucus color. It wavers with the breeze. The branches bend with the fruits' weight. When the fruits fall, they shatter upon striking the ground. They are a pomegranate-quince hybrid, just like the ones on the first tree. The seeds are a brilliant orange. I pluck the seeds out of the meat and place them on my tongue. They burst and it is like drinking ten gallons of juice. My tongue tingles. [Did you even think to save some for me?] Lilith asks me. She eats the root ends and throws the edible parts at me. I dress them with thick oil and sliced garlic. Lilith opens her mouth. Her teeth are pointed. She pulls the Adam man out of the tree trunk and sinks her teeth into his neck. [I got tired of the fruit when I was in the garden,] she says and drinks from him. Lilith craves steak and so I always remember to keep the refrigerator stocked with beef.

There are two Liliths and I do not know which one to side with. Both pull my arms and demand to be fed. [But I cannot give you any more meat than I have. One of you will have to settle on soup,] I say and the Liliths hiss and gnash their teeth. They both want steaks. But I cannot afford to give them enough muscle to settle their carnivorous appetite. The Adam man comes into the world and the women glare at him. They grab his shoulders. [He is my husband,] the first Lilith says. [No, he is mine,] the second Lilith says. They thumb wrestle and breathe fire at each other. The man ducks his head. He grunts and makes terrified squealing sounds. [You are not a pig,] the women shout and the Adam man crawls beneath the carpet. Secretly I roll fruits to him under the floorboards. [If you press them hard enough, you can bring about a compressed fermentation,] I whisper into the carpet fibers. The Adam man chews the hard melon rinds. [I would like to eat some chicken,] he says and I throw raw poultry at his face. He chews slowly and his lips hang past his chin. [I cannot digest all this protein,] he says. He throws the congealed fat away and sobs into the metal floor nails. The women grapple with the remains of the chicken that he did not eat. They steal bites from one another. The first Lilith pulls my hair. [I'm the one who told you about Eden], she says. [The other one is not to be trusted with Adam. She will seduce him away.] The second Lilith watches the first from the corner of her eyes and whispers to me: [I can bring you to the garden.]

And so the second Lilith brings me to the holy garden. The dirt smells acidic. I kick at the many mud mounds and they collapse into ash. The second Lilith slithers up and down a tree. [Isn't it beautiful here,] she says and pulls my hand. I follow her around the garden borders. She hands me metal bushes and a cotton-fiber tree. Every fruit I see is bruised and seeping juice. I keep my arms at my sides, afraid to touch anything. The flowers all have teeth. Their petals brush against my legs and bite into my thighs. In the garden I bleed slowly. This imposter Lilith sits on her branch and giggles as my pants turn bright red from all the flower bites. [Now that is a pity,] she says looking at my pants. The plant roots turn a dark green from my dripping blood. They twine around themselves as they reach towards my wound. [I'm not here to feed you,] I say. The second Lilith climbs onto my shoulders. She leans close to my mouth and says, [But they are relying on you for a food source.] She nips the side of my ear. [That is my mortal, and mine alone,] the first Lilith says, bursting out of a tree trunk. She knocks the second Lilith down and pushes her face into the earth. The second Lilith's face turns to stone. The first Lilith strikes the forehead three times and leaves a crack. The second Lilith's stone face breaks along the fault line and cracks apart. [Paradise isn't meant for everyone, especially not you,] the remaining Lilith says. [It's far too dirty.]

The garden grows up into my window pane. Lilith feeds the weeds from her sliced thumb. Her stomach is still distended from devouring her twin. Adam sits in the kitchen counter, combing his short hair with his fingers. He whimpers and gnaws on the copper pipes. [If we exchange blood one night,] Lilith says to me. [You will develop my disease, but we will be one.] She shows me her black hair and pale white eyes. [I am a dying woman,] she says sadly. She pushes her hands through her throat and removes a bushel of ripe red fruits. She hands me two and keeps the rest for herself. [I'm so tired,] she says. [It is the man. His very presence makes my muscles weak. You can't imagine what we've been through.] She opens the closet and yanks him out of his hiding spot. He curls up in her fist. Lilith cuts his sides open and takes out a pair of his ribs. He doesn't flinch. She swallows the tiny bones. The curving parts jut out against her throat. [He stole these from me when we were younger. I was newly created. I was more liquid than solid. I was more mud than flesh. And he stole my ribs and ate them. But now I have them back. He was never meant to conquer me,] she says. She puts Adam in the sink and washes him of her gold bile. He falls asleep in her fist. Lilith turns to me. [You shouldn't be so ready to go to the garden,] she says. [It is nicer here. You have everything you need. The garden is too... fleshy,] she says. She vomits up a small rib and hands it to me to eat.

Lilith's Vulvodynia – Act Two

Lilith's vagina swelled until her lower body was engorged with the mess of her labia. [But can a goddess have genitals that are so fruitful,] she wondered. So instead she bred her demons. She bred them so that each one had her face. And it was lovely. Their faces looked just like a fruit. This time it was not an Apple, nor a Pomegranate, nor a Grape. Just a generic red fruit. Ripe and smooth. Dripping off the stem. The man came to mate with her. Over his shoulder he carried a bag of his reproductive proteins. [Don't my protcins smell sweet,] he asked. [They smell like sour milk,] Lilith said as she leaned over and vomited. The asylum doctor, who managed the garden, came to her and grappled with her snake hair. [Can I have some fruits,] she asked. The doctor gave her a syringe in her upper arm. [You will get pineapple serum and like it,] he said. [It is the milk of life.] Lilith was allergic to those fruits of the pine tree. They made her twitch and itch. No one came to visit her until noon on the seventh moon. It was Adam who came. He was just as tall and handsome as she remembered. All the children were with him. [My baby,] Lilith said. She showed Adam her vagina. Hot chilies grew out of the canal. The vines were unwieldy. [What about some for my cooking,] Adam asked and pried several long red pepper pieces off. The tearing hurt badly. Lilith screamed and cursed. Then one child put a plastic knife to the throat of another. [Fratricide,] the children sang. [Frat-Ree-Side.] Exhausted by the thought of her children, Lilith dipped her head down and put her mouth to her anus. She shat and ate the chunks. [This is the only way I will get my protein from now on,] she said. [They refuse to give me anything to eat. They tell me that the only protein I can have is from the man's sack. Every meat dish looks like a spider.] Adam dragged Eve's body out from behind the basement walls. [You can devour her and get your protein here,] he said. Lilith sobbed. She tore through the woman's pale shoulders. Her meat was paltry. The doctor, in his long white coat and big beard, stalked forward and seasoned Eve's leathery hide with pills.

Lilith ate the worms out of her vagina. They were thick strings with sacks on the ends. They were like tape worm things. She popped their ends and the tiny monsters blistered. Everything fell apart around her but Lilith kept close to the peeling walls. [What now,] she asked the solitary woman standing near her. When she looked again, the woman was a skeleton. No, she was a fruit tree. Or maybe she was a meat dish. Confused, Lilith sang into the concrete. Her demons fell out. They giggled and bounced on the bed until the bed springs gave in. [I should be so lucky,] she said. [I should be so lucky.] She writhed on the metal coils. She hissed. She broke things. She sucker punched every man that got too close. Adam cried in the garden, [Why won't she love me?] He sobbed and gnats swarmed his head. Lilith kept her hands pressed against his ears so that he couldn't hear her anymore. He listened instead to the seashell beat of his sad head. [Will you visit me every Monday,] she asked and he smiled before nodding, [No]. Then she beat and kicked him. She tore at his genitals. Then she beat his wife. [You will never tell me no,] she shouted and beat him again. So he cried. Buttes came out of her asylum cell. The doctor dove off the cliff face and landed at her feet. [If you are not careful, you will never be well,] he said. He sucked her toes. Lilith giggled. She grabbed her demon tails and swung them around. She knocked the doctor away. [Take your poison with you,] she said. The doctor laughed. He struck her across the backs of her knees. She couldn't walk for days. The straight jacket mocked her by climbing the forbidden tree. [Not fair,] she screamed. The doctor tried to make love to his patient, his ward, his creation, but when he pushed his genitals against hers, her body swelled closed. Her vagina was an engorged thing—a concave balloon. She twisted until his semen drained out of her. Then she spit the fluid at his face. For this he never forgave her.

Oh, pained snake goddess Lilith. She tried to use a vibrator but it made her cry. [You are hysterical,] the nurses said and cranked the shaft back and forth within her until Lilith screamed. [You must not be so loud,] they said. So she throttled her throat and laughed until the nurses quivered. [You know nothing about me,] Lilith said as she wrenched her uterus out. She shook it around inside her fist. The tubes slapped against her wrist. The uterus writhed and ate itself. The doctor smacked the monster with syringes. [The id must be put to sleep,] he shouted. Later, after she had slept for nearly a year and a day, Adam came to visit her. He brought her steaks wrapped in brown paper. [They won't give me any meat,] she complained while chewing the strings of yellow fat. [I know,] Adam said as kissed her once, then fed her the forbidden apple he had hidden in his throat. [The fruit,] she gasped and Adam nodded. [They refuse to give me any fruits as well,] she said. She clawed the walls and the plaster fell out. The concrete landed on Adam's feet, rooting him in place. [If I water you, you might become an apple tree as well,] she said and urinated on his ankles. He did not sprout but soaked and rotted. Lilith giggled. [Do you remember that time in the garden,] she asked.

Adam nodded, pretending he remembered everything. [It was such a fun time,] she said. [Oh yes,] Adam said. [That one time,] Lilith said as she pushed the rocks over his knees and crushed his knee caps. The doctor stood behind her. [It is time to let him go, Lilith,] he whispered. She didn't move. He pulled her off of Adam. The medical man touched Lilith, but she did not like it, not after what he had done. Snakes erupted from her spine. Serpents bit the doctor's hands, tore them into stumps. [In the garden, I strung you up from the tree. And you rotted from the outside in. It was beautiful. Our own living gallows. And you whimpered in the death throes and apples fell from your feet,] he said. [That is why you can't eat the apples. They will remind you of your death.]

During intercourse Lilith burned. It was not a pleasurable pain. [I have tried to open the gates,] she told the men dressed in long black coats. Some took notes. [What gates,] they asked as she frowned. [There were gates,] she said again. [Large gilded gates. Wrought iron. They surrounded the garden. They made a strange noise. A metal sound. They made me sick. I felt disease in my belly. Deep inside, deeper than my bowels. It all felt sticky. So I ate a fruit and that settled everything. I only ate the juice, not the flesh. I sucked the fruit dry, like a spider does. I threw the desiccated body away without remorse or hunger,] she said. [There were no fruits. There is no garden and there are no gates,] the men said.

[You imagined it all.] They brought her to the window of her room and forced her to look out through the iron bars. The grounds were dark. They were made of concrete. A single flower grew up from the sidewalk. It was pale yellow. It had no leaves. There were no fruits. [You never had fruits in the garden,] the men said. Lilith unhinged her jaws and swallowed one of the men's heads. [How can you say that? You do not know my garden,] she screamed. The men injected her arms with tranquilizers. She fell to the ground and sat with her feet behind her ears, scratching. [I thought I was a dog once,] she said. The walls opened. Demons stepped out. They clawed her shoulders. The men stood over her demons, ready with their needles and pills. [Will you let me sleep naturally,] she asked and stuck her tongue out. She took all the medicine they gave her. The demons sat in her throat and swallowed for her. She tasted powder. She tasted bitter. But it was the sort of sweet bitter she enjoyed. It tasted just like the fruit. The demons made love to her and every thrust was like a barbed spine in her vagina. [It hurts,] she said. [It hurts.] The men did not listen. Not until she was pregnant.

[A miracle birth,] the doctors marveled. [We shall perform a necessary hysterectomy.] They stole her womb and left it on the operating table while she slept. [What about my baby demons,] Lilith asked. [They will have to be born another way,] the doctors said. A nurse swallowed the uterus and left Lilith alone with the brick walls. [Where is my apple orchard?] Lilith screamed. She beat her knees against the ground until the marrow from her bones spilled out. Adam emerged from the mess. He smelled of honey. [You are not the man I thought you were,] she said to him. She pulled his ribs out. Huddled inside his chest was the second wife. The Eve woman whimpered and yanked the eyes from her head. She offered them to Lilith. [I thought you might be hungry,] Eve said. Lilith growled. She placed the eyes on her tongue and swallowed. [I now have second sight,] she said mockingly and looked through the walls. The doctors chained her up. Lilith screamed. [Take your womb back. It causes us nothing but trouble,] the doctors said. They forced the womb into her mouth. She gagged. Fertile creatures leaked down her throat and sat just above her shoulders. She coughed and grabbed her throat. [I want them dead,] she screamed as she pointed at the doctors. The doctors strapped her to the bed. She tossed and turned for hours while Adam and Eve watched her. [This is so sad,] they said. They kissed her feet. They ate bricks and spat the ground mortar over her. Every pebble turned into something with a head. Lilith was silenced. She blinked slowly. Her head sank into her torso. [I am a lost soul,] she said. [They have clipped my wings.] Adam turned her over. He stroked the nubs left over from her wings. [My wings were made of the most precious metal but the doctors pawned them,] Lilith said. [There was so much metal, they bought the world. And the apples. And left me nothing.] Defeated, she vomited up a roast loin.

Later, a single child came out of the apple Lilith kept beneath her mattress. It was an apple baby. [Oh, pomegranate seed thing. Hallowed by thy fruit core. As the goddess wills it, so shall it be,] she sang. And when the child sprouted a tree from the top of its head, Lilith rejoiced. It was a good tree. It was a solid structure. The branches reached through the walls and went skyward. [There is no need for wings,] Lilith thought. Proud of her baby, Lilith walked with her head tilted so far that the back of her skull pressed against her neck. It was uncomfortable, but pride makes us do strange things. Lilith barely needed a head. All that the men recognized was her full and voluptuous body. She climbed the stalk. Her outside blistered. Her vulvodynia set in. The skin hung heavily. She dragged it after her. [You will not slow me,] she gasped at her vagina. Ignoring her, her vagina twisted around itself. The Adam man crawled out of it. He rested on her belly and stared up her chin. [You must be in so much pain,] he said. She grappled with the stalk and moved on. The cowardly doctors climbed down the tree. [You must return to your room,] they said. They stripped the plant of its leaves and threw them on the ground. Lilith whimpered. The veins sprouted tiny demons with Adam's heads. [Are you a man? Or are you an entity,] Lilith asked. Adam laughed and zippered his torso. Something moved around his bones. It was slimy. Lilith caught a flash of red. [Is that the apple monster I have heard so much about,] she asked. The cannibal core violently pushed free of Adam's body. It struck her in the face. Blood dripped from the wound. Lilith drank her own blood. She bit her wrists. She tore her ligaments. She was too salty. The doctors threw her into a basket. [You will sit alone in the dark until you calm down,] they said. Lilith sighed. She slapped the men away when they tried to touch her. They fell apart. They were simply bones held together by membranes. Their pelvises each contained a lime. That explained everything.

The goddess's genitals became an ulcer. The doctors cleaned the sores with a hook but that solved nothing. [It hurts whenever you get too close,] she said. Her hands had turned into claws long ago and now, whenever the doctors angered her with their medications, she hit the hooks against them, raking through their skin. She liked how it looked: all the scratches moving from earlobe to throat. [You should keep that adornment permanently,] she said as she cauterized the lines with her breath. The scratches dried to a dull red. The doctors smeared ointment on the scars but no amount of petroleum jelly resurrected the flesh. [Can I have an apple peel?] Lilith asked and the doctors threw up over her clipboard. Not only did they refuse her a single peel, they refused her fruits, and they took her vegetables away, too. She had never wanted a carrot so badly, even though the craving was something new. [I want my fruit. I want my zucchini,] Lilith shrieked and rattled the bars around her room. The walls stood firm. She filed her teeth against the lacquered metal. The doctors tossed meat at her. [Be quiet,] the doctors said. [It's late and all the patients are sleeping.] Lilith growled. She swallowed the meat without chewing. The doctors hit her with sticks until she moved into the corner of her room. Fecal matter was sprayed all over the back wall. [Is this how you would act in your garden,] the doctors asked. Once, Lilith had leaned too close to a toilet bowl and inhaled the toxic cleaning solvents. She imagined the foaming fluid covering her lungs and throat, cleaning every carnivorous impurity stuck to her skin. Then she puked and the chunks came up white. The doctors trapped her in a cat cage. [You can't hurt yourself that way,] they said and Lilith drank glass cleaner spitefully.

An entire room was dedicated to Lilith's vaginal secretions. Bottles of menstrual fluid were confined to one wall while all the jars of cervical mucus stayed close to the other. Lilith salivated over these things. [Where are the children,] she asked. [Where are MY children?] The doctors pointed to the center of the room. There were her egg sacs. There were tissue remnants from her babies. There were jars of assorted eyes. There were tins of mouths. There were other scattered things from her babies as well. Lilith wanted none of them. [Get rid of them,] she said. [You have no right to keep them. Get rid of them.] The doctors swept them into the corners. [No,] she shouted. [I want them gone. I want them gone! I want them gone!] She kicked the jars, tins, and bottles until they shattered. Lilith sat on the ground. She pouted. She pulled cockroaches out of her hair. She threw the heavy backed bugs across the room. They fell into the uterine pieces hanging on the wall and got stuck. [I hate everything,] Lilith sulked. She stuck her lip out and the doctors injected medication into the lower part. [You're being dramatic,] they said. She spit at them. Numbed, the doctors unzipped her torso. Adam came out. [You really are being overly dramatic,] he said. She crawled up to him, dragging her lower part behind her and sighed. Her head rested against the rise of his foot. [Where is your holy Eve? Where is your love,] she asked. [She stayed home,] Adam said. [I hate her,] Lilith said. [You hate everyone,] Adam said. Gently and tenderly, he pulled her hair out of her scalp and wound the strands around his shoulders. [I breathed in things I shouldn't have,] Lilith said. [Terrible foamy things that hurt my stomach. I think I am burned through the inside.] She pointed at her navel. Adam put his nose to the umbilical entrance and stared. [I see nothing but bright red,] he said. Lilith slapped her palms together in glee. [That is the burn,] she shouted. [It's like an apple!]

The doctors brought Lilith to an apple orchard. [Do you see,] they said, pointing. [There is nothing there. Only apples. There is no sacred tree.] Lilith stared. She sniffed the base of each tree. Her feet sank in the mud. She pulled them out and flicked the muck away. [This isn't my garden,] she said. [You don't have a garden, Lilith,] the doctors said. [But I do. It is called Eden. It was my garden. I owned it. I picked apples from it every day,] she cried loudly. To calm her, the doctors injected her arms. They fed her an apple slice. They gave her cups of apple cider. She let the masticated fruit bits drop out of her mouth. The juice dribbled down her breasts. She left a mess on her lap. The doctors injected her arm and dragged her to the largest tree. She carved Adam's face into the trunk. [Can you hear me,] she whispered. [They're trying to tell me that this tree is the tree.] The Adam mouth moved and Lilith clapped her hands. [Tell them,] she said and pointed at the doctors. The doctors sighed. [Tell them,] she said. Adam and the doctors turned into bat-headed demons. They barked and Lilith dropped worms into their mouths. The doctors giggled and ran around in circles, chasing their rattlesnake tails. Her vagina ached, it had been so long. The Adam tree reached into her hole and she burped up polished apple seeds. [It burns,] she said but the doctors refused to listen. They hissed three times and whistled through the hollow in their pointed tongues. Lilith named them after the sins, one by one. She ate blades of grass. She shat out shrubbery. [Is this wrong,] she asked the Adam tree. It shook its branches, NO. [I have inhaled terrible things. And now I am forever burned on the inside,] she said. The tree belched. It shoved fruits up her nose. The skins had a citric acid fragrance. She pulled lemons out of her chin. Seeds fell from her nose.

Even though it was against the rules, Lilith sat on her therapist's lap. [You are better now,] the man asked. Lilith stared at the papers arranged across his desk. The words were connected scrawls of snake tracks. [Can I go outside,] she asked. The doctor patted her wrists. [When you are better, you are free to go,] he said. Lilith climbed onto the window sill. The therapist applauded as she sat on the ledge and looked down. His office was many stories up in the air. She looked at the solid metal cage behind her in the room, the one they had wheeled her in on, and leaped. She fell for hours, then hit the ground. The concrete was soft. It felt like a sponge. She sank into it. She waded through the streets. She sprawled over the sidewalk and breathed the rock. Adam helped her up. [Are you happy now,] he asked. He placed a hand over her backside and inserted three fingers into her vagina. Her vagina ached. Her vagina ached and ate his hand off. [You shouldn't touch me without permission,] she said. Adam stared at the stub of his hand. Lilith put her lips to the wound and waited patiently for a root to sprout. A tree emerged from his arm. [Look,] she said, pointing. [It's an Adam tree!] Every fruit was heavy with Adam's pale face. She aimed darts at the cores and let the juice drain onto the ground. [Oooh,] she said. [Some apples are quite acidic.] She drank the potion up, pebbles and all. Adam winced. His skin peeled off. Lilith ate each slice of flesh before it landed on the road. [They wouldn't feed me, Adam,] she said. [I was hungry and they refused to feed me. They gave me mashed things and bits of meat. You know I don't eat any of that. I am picky.] Adam lost his teeth. Lilith held them in her hand. Her back itched. Her vagina dropped out. She watched it go, scampering down the street. Her spine sprouted. [My wings,] she whispered in delight. [They've grown back.] They opened up, looming over her body. She stepped forward and flew away. Back to her garden.

Silhouettes of a Stricken Eve

I grew from the rib. No. I sprouted from the rib. Then I burrowed. The man thought I was a parasite. The Eden worm. An Evemoeba. He vomited me up and I splashed on the ground. I became bone and marrow dripped out of my mouth. The man gave me his hand and I bit him with the razor bones pushing out of my skull. But this was long ago. First, there was a rib, then Adam, claiming that I sneaked into his torso and pulled all the pieces out for myself. This is not true. The pieces were a gift. I was a rib, then the angel hands gave me a shadow face. It took months before I could see myself in a pool of water. Before that I was just dust. The water splintered off from the clouds and left tiny bones everywhere. The bones cut through Adam. They cut him, not me. I bit Adam. I devoured him. I devoured him first, then the tree. The red fruits burst over my face. They stained the bone bright scarlet. I pulled at the ribs. They broke.

But I was not a rib. I was never a rib. I was a breast. A bone. A breast bone. A mammary gland with a woman's face sewed to the nipples. I hung in midair, hanging from the chest. Adam swatted at the breastly me with his chest. He broke my throat in half and it took many days for the hole to heal. The angels filled the space with loose feathers and tiny mounds of yellow fat. I was allergic to the yellow fat. When they stuffed me with it, I swelled to five times my own weight. Then the tree fell over. I was crushed under it. But eventually I was born again. Just as I had been promised. I was born and the Adam man offered me a branch. A branch of peace. The wood was attached to a rubber sternum. The more he urged me towards his chest, the more open my neck became. The angels seeing my starvation fed me raw meat. They said I was an animal. There had been a wife before me and the angels were afraid I would turn out like her. I saw her in the desert, chewing stripped bones while picking the sand from her eyes. I placed the meat over my breasts and let it rot.

Adam's Wood. It fell out of the sky. It was like Cedar planks. I was like a blue fin tuna—all fishy on the inside. The Adam man cut me in half. He gave his wood to the tree and turned away while the trunk ate. Its branches chewed slowly. They broke the fiber down into a thick pulp. [Paper face,] I thought. I wanted to eat from my knees. I wrote my memoirs using marrow as ink. Adam touched my face. [The longer I look at you, the more you fade away,] he said and placed his palm to my cheek. His hand pushed through my jaw bones. I splintered. I became a gas that touched ant heads and turned the eyes into calcified stones. [Will I become a bone?] I asked the air. I bit into a tree and stayed rooted to the spot for over five years. Adam traveled the world without me, then he came back. His feet were gone. He smelled of cedar wood. His ankles were a blistered red. [My first wife ate from me,] he said and showed me the fang marks on his shoulder blades. Each bit foamed with thick yellow gelatin.

Then things became dust. Dirt. Powder. I touched my finger to my teeth. The enamel crumbled and piled at my feet. I pressed my tongue to the dust. The tip fell to the ground. [Those were valuable taste buds,] Adam said. [You should be careful.] I tasted banana. It was bitter. Unripened. My ankles fell off. [My first wife could keep her entire body together,] Adam said. He vomited stacks of raw skirt steaks and chewed them up. We turned bright green together. [Do you miss the wilderness of the garden?] Adam asked. My wrists were thick with dust chains. I dragged them on the ground. My genitals ruptured. But no fluid came out. Instead, it was a cloud of grit. The sand covered everything. It burned my thighs. I brushed it off but the soil thickened. It created a thick dark skin. Adam picked through my elbows.

There were marrow bugs inside. Little ants made of gristle. They chewed my flesh until I was riddled with holes. Adam's wood grew. Adam planted sprigs of his hair in the ground and they sprouted.

I sank into the sand. Then into the dirt. Adam stuck his hands into the ground. He fished out bits of me. I slipped through his finger. I was like water. He could not catch me. I clung to his skin, then I dropped off. [Freedom,] I thought. Being made of sand kept me drifting away from him. I traveled away from the garden. I slipped up a mountain. I entered a cave. I fell apart in a river. Adam's first wife gathered me up from the river. She found every grain of me and placed them on her lap. [I'm afraid of you,] I said. Lilith laughed. She pressed her tongue against me. I lifted up. [I could swallow you. And that would be the end. Goodbye, little Eve,] she said. But she did not eat me. [Let the stories show that no matter what, Lilith never destroyed the precious Eve,] I thought aloud. She placed me on her breast bone. She had one too. I breathed with her. [The Adam man will wear me down,] I said. Lilith picked me up on her fingertips. She blew at each grain that I was. I drifted with the breeze. I undulated down river and became a pebbled crested tide pool.

Adam was a man. Adam was a monster. He was a vegetable. Maybe he was a carrot. No. He did not have enough orange to his skin. I could not peel him. Not even with a sharp branch. He was no carrot, he was an onion. He made my eyes water. I cried every time I cut him. His cells mashed down, turning into a thick clear gelatin that covered my hands and left my arms itching for days. I tried to peel Adam once while he was asleep. I used my nails. I bit them until they were razors. I had steel hands. Adam's hands were simply dumb stone. I peeled him and each layer of his skin was dried paper. He rustled and cracked. I broke his skin. He was brittle. Adam was an insect. Adam was a worm. He had three heads and he crawled on his belly. He tried to live in my digestive tract, but there was not enough room for him in there. He went down my throat and I gagged. I nearly died as I spat him out. Then Adam sat on the ground and waited for me to step on him. When I did, he pushed his head into my foot. He climbed up the inside of my leg. My leg veins ruptured and turned violet. They ached when I walked so I grew wings.

I landed on Adam. I spread my legs. I twisted my arms. I placed my mouth over his head. I grew across his shoulders. I. I. I. I, I, I, I. Everything was always about me. There would be no Adam if there was no Eve. No Adam without me. This is why everything was always about me. Once, Adam tried to convince me to use we. [We,] he said. [Not I.] I did not want to be a part of him. I did not want to be part of we. So I grew a hard shell and climbed into a fruit. The sticky juice clung to my skin. Stinging insects bit me. They shat fruit peels into my eyes. Syrupy pulp bubbled out of my mouth. Adam collected the syrupy juice in a glass. He drank all the fluid. His lips turned blood red. Afterward, everything he ate tasted distinctly of rotten tuna fish. My spine planted itself in the palms of his hands. The vertebrae spread through his fingers until he developed advanced arthritis. The digits twisted. He became a gnarled old man while the spine petals pushed out of my shoulders. As my spine blossomed, his back bent. My tongue was pollinous.

I did not grow a mask. I did not turn into Eve. Not until the ribs were stolen away from me. Not until Adam fell to his knees, genitals in hand and begged for mercy. Then I ate him. I tore apart his arms and legs. I left his torso intact. He raised his arms in mercy towards his first wife. She looked over my head as if she couldn't see him. Instead she swathed me in a black veil. The veil was beautiful. The fabric was inky, silky, filmy, and light. I looked through it and everything was shrouded in delicate gray. Adam looked sad. I pulled a fruit from my cut breasts and fed it to him. His jaw splintered as he chewed. His teeth fell out of his head. [There will be childbirth in this new world,] he cursed and I patted him on the throat until he swallowed. He was just a slab of meat. And I was just a flat shadow. I laid my chest across his and he bled while I spread myself across the trunk of the forbidden tree. [I will always love you,] I said but he smelled strongly of rotten onions. Lilith halved him, then she quartered him.

I splashed and Adam drowned. He drowned in his nasal passages. I swam in my urine stream. Adam stuck his nose into a fruit bowl. I let a handful of blood drain down my throat. Fluid filled our lungs and we turned pale from the effort of breathing. Adam was bluer than I. He was the color of frozen ice. I bathed him in warm water when he was asleep and a half-liquid slush poured out of his spinal cord. Adam didn't know that his vertebrae were on the verge of melting. He touched himself between the legs and the first lumbar bones disintegrated. [Doesn't the Adam man realize that self-gratification is a no-no in Eden?] Lilith asked. Her hands were buried up to the wrist in her mons pubis. Water drained out of them both. Her water was paler. His had dark specks. [Do they have a flavor?] I asked before tasting. Adam sneezed. The water ran out of his nose. I drank from his mouth. He tasted like vinegar. I drained him into the quicksand earth. [It is better this way,] I thought.

Then we were away from the garden. We were expelled. Now there were stone walls, and a rock canopy. [It's called a ceiling,] Lilith said as she patted my wrists. Our heartbeats echoed each others. Adam stayed outside, behind a molding door. He was afraid to come inside. He still wore ivy leaves around his waist. They were the poison variety and scratched his genitals, spreading the rash across his abdomen. Lilith scraped the red scales clean and fed them to her pet demons. They looked like three-headed cats. I fed them fruits when they barked. [What is down the hallway?] I asked. Lilith pointed to the stones. I carved my face into the sides. She added hers. The images pressed together, side by side. They were conjoined, half-faced solar entities. Adam couldn't tell us apart. [Lilith,] he wondered. [Eve?] We answered in the same voice. [Yes, Adam,] we replied. Then he stuck dirt into his mouth and chewed, drowning us out. We took turns licking him into submission.

Lilith, Mother - Act Three

This woman had wings. In the earth goddess's terrain stomach, this woman grew like a tulip, unfurling her arms like petals and stabbing them through the roots. Her roots went deep. The gravity here was nothing like what she had experienced before. Forget Deuteronomy. She did not believe in endings. She only believed in her own name—the black flower, the thorny rose, the Lilith with agate eyes. The Adam man called her name often. [Lilith,] he said. [Lilith, Lilith, Lilith] until her tongue foamed at the tip and she swallowed it back. [How far have I come from Genesis to the New Testament,] she wondered. She was lost between a few pages. She came apart, wilted and dried, losing petal after black petal when the book turned inside out. She couldn't help those things then: the runny scrambled eggs and the forbidden fruit mashed into the ground to form a muddy paste. [Who would condemn me for that,] she asked. Certainly

fig leaves.

the Adam man would, walking naked with a dead snake fastened around his neck, dangling down to between his legs, grimacing whenever the sun came out. That was not her problem. She was always telling him that, but what did he know? What did she know? Hadn't they just arrived? She stuck her head into the dirt pretending to be a mythological ostrich and breathed pebbles until she was numb. Then she sat up and thought the world spun on its axis so quickly the revolutions were again off-center. Maybe they were. She wanted to take a flight across the galaxy but was afraid of aging alone. Or not aging alone. Or feeling immortal. So that when she came back, the earth was a planet of gravestones and mausoleums. [What then,] she wondered. She would commit the rest of her life to praying for each corpse, giving out flowers at their funerals and recalling the anniversaries of their deaths. Days of birth, virginal passings, and professional suicides, she would strive to remember them all. But she would be the only one; no one else would remember those sacrifices. So she would go back into space and convince a series of galaxies to consume one another. Celestial crusades would be her calling. It would be fun. She would laugh a lot, like in a game. A game with missing puzzle pieces and glued felt leaves. Her secret was simple: she would place a layer of needles in between the pieces of fabric, and if anyone twisted the felt leaf too hard one way or the other, that player would get cut. It would be her revenge. Something Lilith had wanted to do to Adam a long time ago. Instead she had to settle for cutting him with broken coconut shells while he slept. He thought the black bruises meant that he had started turning into stone. God had promised him those little things. Things like angel wings when he could no longer stand, and granite ankles that would never break. God promised him these things during his brief brush with immortality. God did this because the angelic should be heavy.

She thought about selling herself to other men. It was a banana peel decision—quick and slippery. Instead it turned out to be klutzy. All she knew was that it would be better than sleeping with Adam all the time. At least she would get something out of it. Her hair would become tough like a bird's nest and nothing would hurt her. Then she thought about selling Adam instead. Of offering him to an eagle or some sort of mountain priest that would shun the female body but embrace the male. [A mortal angel,] she could say. [One of flesh and not stone.] Adam would surely have nightmares when not in his lover's arms. Or his rapist's arms. She didn't know anymore. She barely knew her own name—Lilith. Lilith sat down and pondered the meanings of the nominal world. [Why is the sky named the sky and not water? Why does water signify liquid,] she wondered. Perhaps all the things she thought of as animals were actually people; she and Adam might be the only animals in the entire world. The more she thought, the more sand spilled out of her ears. It was red sand. A rare variety. One that was made of semi-precious stones—rubies—crushed against a woman's thigh and ground down with gleaming white bone. A sand that would squeak when rubbed between the molars. To get such precious red sand, Lilith needed a mortar and pestle, and maybe even a few minutes with the empty basin of Adam's opened skull. She looked at him and saw that his flesh was still intact. She had nothing to look forward to—maybe a sunrise or two, the expansion of the fetal wings in her spine, or maybe even a rise of her shoulders. She would still like to grow spines, spikes, horns, all over her body. This way when Adam got too close—Prick! No more Adam and she would be free. If he got pricked he wouldn't be dead, not right away. He would be decorated with puncture wounds all over, writhing on his belly on the ground like a man snake. Lilith could then look down at him, squirming and squirming and scream, [Look out! It's a sand man! It's a sand worm! Oh, oh look. A snake man.] Sand would pour out of his body. He would hemorrhage sand. He would spew sand. Then Lilith would pour water over his head and wash his body across Eden and watch it disintegrate. Thinking about this, Lilith felt her wings kicking within her back. She groaned and rotated her hips to face back. Sometimes she felt like a puzzle piece. She never began as a whole entity. She was simply a series of splinters striving to make up a forest. Adam could be a part of that piece of wood, but she would never allow it.

Lilith's head was a monolith, a necropolis, a monument to false gods and gold idols. She ate apples rich with severed worms and bits of snake tail. When the Adam man stood by her, he gnawed tree bark studded with orange peels and cloves. [It's a Cajun thing,] he said and waited for the skies to pour chicory coffee into his open mouth. His lips were monsters. They yawned and dripped venom over her. His mouth was an angry mouth; it was rabid. There was foam on his tongue. Lilith was convinced that if she got his saliva on her, she would become something like him. A brute of a woman. Or worse, a nothing woman. A shadow woman. A puppet woman. He would dangle her strings from branches and make her hop and jump whenever he stuck out his tongue. If he wanted, he would make her shake this way and that. He would make her have sex with trees and with animals. She would be forced to call his name out in pleasure. In reality, all she wanted to do was teethe on the strings until they snapped in two. Lilith imagined the dirt as a sledgehammer. She wanted to take Adam's head and strike it hard against the ground. She wanted to hit him harder and harder until his bones broke beneath her fists. But she was afraid. She was not ready to feel blood on her hands. Adam stirred behind her.

She turned around slowly, unwillingly. He held a sharpened flint in his hand. [We will sacrifice you,] he said.
He lashed out with the stone. She tried to back away
but his arm was longer than she thought. The stone
caught her between the legs and dug into her flesh. She
screamed. Her flesh puckered and furrowed. It turned
shades of brown, red, pink, and white. She gasped and
touched her hands to the gash. Blood collected in the
palm of her hand. The flint sliced again. It was not a flint;
it was a snake's head. She grabbed the snake's head from
Adam's hand and shoved it in her mouth. She bit down
as hard as she could, grinding the stone down with her
teeth until it was pulverized. Her body ached. Her blood
flowed out of her. It mixed with the dirt and made mud.
Adam shook his head and turned his back on her. [And
the Lord, God, said that the woman should bleed once a
month for as many days as the creation took,] he quoted.
The blood flowed and dried. Her pelvis pulsed with an
inner pain. She imagined a drum beating within her. She
struck the metal rims. She beat her fists against the drum
itself. Dum, dum, dum, dum. When she tired, she slowed
the drumming down to a tap. Tap, tap, tap, tim, tim, tim,
rat a tat, rat a tat, rat a tat tat. She knew she could perfect the drum. The drum doubled so Adam could play
as well. She stuck her foot through both drum cylinders.
No instrument would betray her, not one that she could
play so well.

Lilith imagined the Adam man longing for a partner to lie beneath him. He was a heavy man and she did not want to be burdened by the addition of his weight. She sat on the ground despite her bleeding. She would make Adam a different partner. First, she sewed mushrooms together, taking care to use the poison variety for both the head and genital glands. But the body was too fungal. It smelled too strongly of musk and made her feel ill. She felled one thousand oak trees and entwined their branches. But the body was too green for Adam's taste. He would get lost in the leaves. He would be injured by the many knots. Despite her wanting to hurt him, Lilith preferred the pain to be emotional. She ate the entwined trees before midnight and pulled all the splinters from her tongue, throwing the pieces of wood onto a pile that grew until it nearly touched the moon. Perhaps she could give Adam a celestial body to abuse. She might be able to give him the moon or another planet, a star, or some cold entity like a comet that would give him frostbite. She could also give him something so warm that he would burn when trying to have his way with it. Lilith jumped up and down, trying to reach something celestial but she could not; they were too far away. When she was halfway to the moon, it opened its mouth and bit the tips of her fingers off. Lilith cried over her severed fingers. She touched the missing flaps of skin and frowned. The moon spit the flesh onto her and she brushed the pieces out of her hair. The flesh melted into her shoulders. Lilith burned all over. She realized her thighs were wet with blood. The droplets dripped down her legs and puddled around her feet, soaking into the earth. Using the soiled mud, she molded a woman. She gave her small breasts and delicate hips. She gave her woman a slender body. She was petite. Tiny. Something Adam could use. Something Lilith could crush if angered. When she stared at the figure, she was convinced that the woman was more of a girl. [What have I done?] Lilith whispered. [If you were grown, I would not feel so guilty. But you are a child? I have created you to be destroyed.] She sobbed as the child awoke and looked around. [What am I,] the child asked. Lilith brushed the girl's mud hair out. [You are a woman,] she said. [I feel much younger,] the child said. [Do I have a name? Do I have a mother,] she asked. [You are newly born,] Lilith said. [I am your maker. I will name you Eve.] The child rubbed her eyes. [What do you want me for,] she asked. Lilith patted her head gently. [You will love my husband for me,] she said and took hold of the child's arm to lead her.

Lilith gave birth to a child. The labor was long. She gasped and screamed for three full moons while Adam and the girl huddled together, covering their ears to silence Lilith's screams. Lilith ate poison mushrooms as she labored, shoveling the brightly colored pieces into her mouth. She vomited them up immediately and beat her hands against her stomach to push the baby out. She touched between her legs and was stung by something hiding inside. Bending forward, she noted a scorpion tail pushing past her genitals. It stung the air repeatedly, the sharp bulb on the end glistening with venom. Lilith whimpered. Her fingers swelled. She felt the child crown. Eve screamed and pressed her face against Adam's chest. He held her tightly. They both looked away from Lilith. The scorpion stung her inner thighs. When not stinging her, the scorpion pricked the infant's head. The moon descended and picked Lilith up. [It is an angel,] Adam said and fell to his knees. Eve followed him but struck the ground too heavily. Blood welled up from the scrapes on her knees. [It hurts,] Eve moaned. Lilith gasped. The moon's hands were colder than she had expected. The fingers left blue marks on her body. Lilith whimpered and felt the moon's hands slip between her legs. The fingers pulled at the baby's head. She pushed and pushed. The moon hummed a single note. [Will you make me a stone?] Adam asked, looking at the moon. The baby slid free. The moon held it up by one foot. Lilith stared at her child. It was swathed in a black caul. [I am afraid to look inside the swaddle,] she said. The moon pulled the shroud aside. The baby was faceless. Lilith gasped. Eve crawled forward. [I want the baby. Please, give me the baby,] she gasped. [You will have your own child one day. This one is mine,] Lilith said. Eve grabbed for the baby.

The moon held the baby away. Eve bit the moon's bottom and the baby dropped. Eve opened her mouth, revealing the white phosphorescence smeared across her tongue and lips. She grabbed the baby and cuddled it to her bosom. The baby opened its mouth and latched onto Eve's dry breast. It suckled quietly. [It loves me,] Eve said. [I am a mother.] She sighed and held the child close. Lilith reached for the child, pleadingly. [It is mine,] she said. [No. I want one. You already birthed me. I have nothing to take care of,] Eve said. Adam finally stood. [Our first child,] he said to Eve. He kissed the girl's forehead. Lilith screamed. Wings sprang from her back. Deep within her, the scorpion hissed and snapped its tail. [I will steal everything from you,] she said and rose into the air.

Lilith imagined a palace of stone and crystal. She envisioned that the crystals would be made entirely of salt. She would eat the salt, shard by shard, rock by rock, until her body dried up from the inside out. There would be every variety of salt: black, pink, white. Even strange shades of yellow-green and purple. Some would be too salty for her tongue. Others would be so mild; they could be mistaken for sugar grains. She would live in this palace, surrounded by the salt, and think nothing of the outside world, nothing of Adam. Lilith dreamed that Adam would be interred in a casket made of polished mica. She would stand over him and sob into her hands. He was not a bad man. He had made mistakes.

But she could forgive him in death. The last thing she remembered was Adam opening his eyes. He opened his mouth. His tongue slid past his lips. On the tip was a small fruit. A red fruit. By the way the flesh bulged; Lilith knew the fruit had many seeds. [Eat the fruit,] Adam said in a muffled voice. She took the fruit off of Adam's tongue and bit into it. She rolled the fruit around in her mouth. It was not sweet. She tasted notes of meat, and possibly too much salt. There was a citrus undertone as well. But no sugar. The fruit was not even juicy. She spit the piece out. It landed in Adam's mouth. He swallowed the fruit. Lightning flashed. Adam closed his eyes. [The Lord said not to eat the forbidden fruit,] he said. Lilith's eyes teared. [You tricked me,] she said. [I simply offered,] he said. He opened his mouth again and she saw how the insides were now a fermented brown. A moldy green color covered his gums. Adam smelled sickly. [No worry,] he said. [I will die before you. In fact, that is how the Lord will curse you. You will live forever.] His lips sewed themselves shut and became a single piece of discolored, calloused flesh. Eve crawled out of his nostrils. She was bloodied and naked. When Eve lifted her head, Lilith could see that the girl had no throat. When Lilith woke up, she was lying on cold sand. There was no castle made of crystal salt. There was no Adam and no Eve. They were together in the garden without her. They were with the fruits, lusting after the seemingly perfect flesh, not knowing that the meat inside was barely enough to appease their hunger. Lilith stretched her limbs. The scorpion between her legs snapped. She chewed on her bottom lip and waited for the moon to lift her up. Her wings were tired. Their iron was beginning to rust.

She became a snake. An iron snake. A gold snake. A silver and a jade snake. A naked snake with wings. A monster snake and a feather snake. A poisonous snake and a harmless snake. She was a mean snake. She became a snake and slid back into Eden, where she came across Adam and Eve sleeping. They snored into one another's mouths. Lilith wrapped the length of her body around their throats and squeezed tightly until their snores were silenced. When she relaxed, they immediately snored again. Lilith hissed. She slid up the tree and coiled around the many branches. She was a loa woman. She was a goddess serpent. Men and women would worship her form. They would give her different names. There was the Lilith of Eden and the Lilith of the desert. The serpent Lilith and the demon Lilith. She laughed and the echoes woke the woman up. Eve approached the tree. [Mother,] she asked. [Is that you? I can barely remember what you look like. Please, come free of the tree. I am afraid of the man. He cannot be satiated. My hips ache from his demands. Where did you go?] Lilith dropped down and hissed. The girl did not move. [My Eve,] Lilith said. [Aren't you hungry? Have an apple. It will make you strong.] Her tail descended, a perfect apple cradled in the center of its coil. The fruit dropped into Eve's outstretched hands. Lilith smiled at her child. [You must eat the fruit before the man awakes, or else he will steal it from you. He does not want you to gain strength or knowledge. He wants everything for himself. That is why he forces you to lie beneath him,] Lilith said. Eve ate the fruit: peel, flesh, seeds, and core. She swallowed the stem whole and grimaced. [It tastes so bitter,] she said. Lilith smiled. Adam shouted. He ran to the tree. Lilith's scorpion hissed and snapped the air. She shook her snake tail and rattled the tree. Apples fell to the ground. Eve turned around, blocking his view of the serpent. [You should have a fruit,] she said and pointed to the many fruits on the floor. [The Lord said we must not eat of that tree,] Adam said. [But the fruits are no longer in the tree. Thus, you can eat what is now of the ground,] Eve said. Adam looked around and saw that Eve was right. The fruits were not of the tree, they were of the ground. He stooped over and took a fruit into his hand. His was polished slate. He bit into the fruit. Seeds stuck in his teeth. Lilith slipped back up the tree. Her limbs grew. Adam ate the fruits noisily as she resumed her normal shape. Lilith climbed to the very top of the forbidden tree. She spread her wings and flew away.

Then there was no Lilith. There was no Adam and Eve. There were simply two couples with two-half faces, staring out and seeing nothing. Lilith was split in half. Her double was Samael. Lilith had one breast and half a vagina. Samael had one nipple, one scrotum, and a penis. Adam and Eve was constructed the same way. But whereas Adam and Eve was content to sit in the garden and count fruit trees, Lilith and Samael wanted only pleasure. The female hand touched the male body and the male hand touched the female body. There was a frenzied stroking of breast and genital. The man spurted from his genitals and the woman took the substance and inserted it into hers. Her half womb sprouted with his seed. The man was wracked with labor pains as Lilith pushed and pushed. She gave birth to quintuplets, five three-headed monsters. The children grew up in only an hour's time, then ran away from them, hiding in the forest. Lilith and Samael wished they could kiss together. They had two tongues that they would push together when feeling passionate, though their lips were attached at the center. They wanted to feel each other's weight but that was impossible. Lilith found an angel who gave her a knife. When the Samael side fell asleep, she took the blade and ran it down their center. While the surgery was painful, the knife cut effortlessly. The blade slid in her hand from all the blood. But finally, the two halves were separated. Lilith was half a woman and Samael was half a man. They made love as best they could, their newly cut edge bleeding and tender. Adam and Eve watched Lilith and Samael struggle. [Could we be like that, too,] the Eve half asked. The Adam half was uncertain. [Perhaps. But it looks so painful,] he said. They stood up and ran towards a small tree. The trunk split them in half. Their bodies fell to the ground, where they lay for a time trembling. There was blood everywhere. Lilith and Samael made love again and again, each time getting a bit better at it. Soon Lilith was giving birth after every climax. The creatures started small and shriveled but became more and more hideous as her climaxes grew. Samael nursed them all on his dry nipple so that Lilith could rest. Seeing all these babies, the Adam and Eve halves came towards them. Adam held the blade that had cut Lilith and Samael in his hand. Inflamed with envy, he stabbed the blade through Samael's neck as Samael coddled his babies. Lilith screamed. The last of her children slid out of her. [These children were to be ours. They are blaspheme. I promise I will do battle with one hundred of your children every day,] Adam said as he slaughtered the children huddled around their birthing mother. [I will drown the same amount of yours,] Lilith wheezed and pushed her final child out. She leaned over and ate Samael's dead body. She ripped the child from Eve's barely swollen womb and threw it into a well. She wanted to drown it, but it did not die. It was a son for Adam.

Lilith craved the meat of men. She craved Adam

and his son. She wanted to eat their bodies whole, then have them deep within her. She watched Adam's son as he slept. The man had a red mark upon his forehead from where she had cracked his skull on the rim of the well. The mark looked much like a cross atop a serpent's back. Lilith sneaked towards him and kissed the mark gently. [Will you come with me,] she asked. Cain nodded as she led him away. Her flesh was cold. She pulled the flesh of his forehead and stripped him of his skin in a single tug. His skeleton rattled loudly. Lilith ate his skin and made love to the skeleton. It struggled to stay together as it pulsed against her. Within moments, it sprayed its seed into Lilith. Lilith laughed and with each laugh she gave birth to five thousand skeletal babies. The children gnashed their fangs and ran up their father's bony legs. They bit his rib cage and pelvis. They ate the last of the flesh covering his body. They consumed the bone. Soon, Cain was nothing. It didn't matter. The fated brother was already dead. Lilith kissed her skeletal children and waved goodbye. [Let Adam kill these babies, for they are his grandchildren,] she whispered. They marched into the distance, disappearing into the forests. A flock of vultures descended from the sky and picked the tiny skeletons that were either too slow or too fat, off the ground. Several of the children were gobbled by the vultures while in the air. The others were bashed against the rocks until their bones jarred loose, allowing the vultures access to warm marrow. [Some will surely survive,] Lilith thought as she slid back into the garden, where she found Adam lying naked on a large black rock. She touched his throat with her fingernails and whispered. Her wings tapped against the small of her back. She kissed Adam gently. [I've missed you, Husband,] she said. He woke up. [My Lilith,] he whispered. [Your son is dead. My children, our grandchildren, ate him,] she said. Adam did not answer. She ran her fingernails along his back and pulled at his spine. The flesh came free easily. She swallowed the skin without chewing. Adam's bones shook and rattled. She rolled the skeleton onto its back and climbed on top. They made love without feeling anything. Adam groaned, filling her with his seed and came apart, bone by bone. Lilith stared up at the heavens and thought of stone caverns and flocks of demons rising out of the sunrise. When he was done, she gave birth again. The children had heads that were simply featureless stones. The limbs were elongated and muscular. Adam grimaced at the sight. Lilith swallowed his body without a second though and spit the remains out at the forbidden tree.

The woman could replace her eyes. The God had felt guilty that she had not been allowed to close her eyes. She could always see the deaths of her children—the ones that were picked off by the vultures and the wild creatures, the ones that were stabbed by holy men, the ones that were drowned, and the ones that were shunned. All the deaths were hers to witness. They made her feel weak. She hated the pained look on her children's faces. They had no fathers. Only a single mother who loved them all. She sacrificed one hundred a day so that she could live and give birth to more children. Adam's seed was still good. And so the God told her she could take her eyes out and place new ones in. At first, the replacements ached. The stones had to be perfect circles of just the right size or else they rotated in her eye sockets. She took to choosing different styles of stone: unpolished circles of amethyst and quartz, balls of feldspar and agate. Some of the stones were painted with blood and natural dyes so that she could enhance the colors. Sometimes her vision was blurry. The stones had to be translucent enough so that she could see properly. Some were too dense and so her vision retained a strange veil. A shadow. A permanent wraith stalking her. Still, she adjusted. The stones occupied her time. She forgot about her many children. She forgot how many were naked and bloodied when she found them. How many had forgotten her name, the name of their mother, while they babbled gibberish and spit up black foam that caused solid earth to disintegrate into a thick pool of liquid. The God had taken pity on her. It had taken him long enough. He had given her the wings but also an unquenchable desire for her first husband. She couldn't stop coming back to him, even after she made him a woman to replace her. He owed this freedom to her. The God did. And maybe Adam did as well. They were his children after all. They both owed her this freedom. Now she could take her eyes in and out whenever she wanted. She could put in bright white stone when she mourned and deep black stone when she hunted. She could make her eyes flash red and she could make them so dull that it seemed as though she had none. Sometimes she placed metal in her eyes so that she was the fiercest goddess in existence. Nothing could penetrate her iron hide. She was stronger than anyone. She was the woman. She was the Lilith. The night spirit. The eater of children. It was not by choice. These were the things she was condemned to as a young goddess. But now, the God was making things right, beginning with her replaced vision. She could not give back her appetites or forget that her first creation had stolen away the first child born of her loins, her only son. But now she had her own eyes. She knew what to look for. She knew everything she wanted to see. From now on, the stories would be hers to tell.

PART THREE

MY
CANNIBALISM

Men, Eggs

The men who sunk their claws into me, swung me around and made a mess of my bones, practiced running their hands up and down my hips all the while screaming, [We have seen into the depths of you and while we were uncertain we would like anything we saw, we now agree that we do. If you will let us deep into your stomach, we will be glad to reach our arms down your throat and wriggle our fingers around in the acid you keep trapped in your gullet. But we will only do that if you promise not to burn the tips of our fingers. We know you are often angry with us for being cruel but we do not mean to be cruel, it is only that we do not really love you but we feel badly about telling you that truth so we try to push you away or show you that you are just another body for us to take advantage of. Sometimes though, gullets dry out, then the acid flakes away and if you have no more acid, tell us now, because we do not want to waste time exploring substances that have been depleted of all caustic identity. If we cannot run the risk of singeing our fingers off in your acid, then what is the point of reaching? Still we do not want to be burned by anything that is part of you, so you must drink an excess of water until we are no longer in any danger and did you know that we treat active digestive systems as a sort of erupting volcano?] If it is volcanoes that they want, then I will give them volcanoes and lava and period blood. If the men are so hungry for things red and stuffed with liquid magma, then I will gladly empty myself, my gullet, my uterus, into a blender for them to enjoy while I suffocated, then mutilated, then burned them away to the point of ash and sunburn.

This wish of mine has nothing to do with men because all the men I loved decayed until they were skeletons. They weren't even lucky enough to be yellow skeletons. Instead they were yellow because the gangrene got them and they spent the last days of their lives vomiting jaundice over everything until the world obtained a yellow hue that made my vision tremble while I batted circulating headaches away. I always think jaundice sounds like such a pretty color even though it is the same shade of postpartum depression wallpaper. Remember this: Nothing lurks within the wallpaper—but when it does, it only has gums wet with saliva.

Once upon a time, I stole fifteen eggs from five men. Either each man owned three eggs or the eggs were scattered amongst them. The first egg cracked until it was a pair of breasts and the second egg cracked to reveal a vagina and the third egg was just a belly button and the fourth egg was an ugly face and the fifth egg was yellow paint which I smeared across my shirt to enhance the color in my cheeks. The sixth egg hatched into a severed wing and the seventh egg dissolved into yolk and the eighth egg was a lost penis finally found and the ninth egg was a skeleton key and the tenth egg was just an egg filled with spring water. I was very thirsty so I sipped it. The eleventh egg was empty and the twelfth egg contained a miniature radiator and the thirteenth egg was just a floor tile and the fourteenth egg was a cross-section of the small intestine and the fifteenth egg was a sliver of rancid bacon. By that point I was so hungry by all the eggs that I ate everything up and I had to have my stomach pumped at the hospital, though the doctors were very nice about it.

The men used to waddle. They were used to throwing their weight around, which meant that their muscles stiffened over time, and so when they walked, they kept their knees jutting out diagonally and their arms levitated inches away from their sides. I tried to push their arms down but I needed more weights than I could carry and so I just ironed the flesh flat and hoped steam heat would do the rest. Sometimes, when the men walked on tiptoe, they rose up so high that their calves split, then

their ankles cracked, and finally, their shins slid right off
their legs and drained into a grass patch that should have
been mowed but was systematically neglected. Then they
were forced to treat their legs like mummies, wrapping
the skin so tightly that they couldn't wriggle their toes
and thus suffered from a weakened cardiovascular system and an odd purple-black stain that ran the lengths
of their soles. Sometimes the men developed metal crav-
ings and couldn't stop lurching towards anything made
of iron: a radiator, a metal bathtub, a pot belly stove, a
water heater, a microwave, a piece of sheet metal, a cast
iron pipe, and even a mattress spring coil. They ate iron
until their stomachs burst from so much material packed
into the acid pools in their stomachs. Then they suffered
acid reflux for the next fifteen days. It makes sense: fifteen days of reflux for fifteen eggs, even though these
men might have been different than the ones who gave
up their ova.

Later, much later, when the yellow postpartum wallpaper began to fade and all the men came out of hiding
with the latex masks still adhered to their faces, I thought,
[What if I made a mistake and all those men really did
love me but I was so desperate to think they were lying
that I shattered their vertebrae without having a reason
to and so they will always be paralyzed from the waist
down unless I feed them to someone who eats humans
but then I would be aiding and abetting a cannibal which

is both a crime against the victims and against human nature and I never want to get in trouble for that so maybe I should just send them to sea where they can learn to float on the white crests of waves like mermen, then I'll be able to see a mermaid for the first time in my life because what mermaid would be able to resist a fresh merman. But what if there aren't any mermaids and as I watch the men floundering around pretending to be mermen with just their arms flapping in the water, they drown and I'm not a good enough swimmer to save them and so they get eaten by a shark. On the one hand, I would be happy that a shark was fed, but on the other hand, I would be sad that I fed these men to a shark, because although they made mistakes they weren't horrible men. What if they've made mistakes because they're human? Haven't I made an equal amount of mistakes, like shunning the ones who loved me and mistaking the intentions of the ones who didn't? The wallpaper was much too yellow, even as faded as it is I thought I would be sick if I had to stay close to this yellowness any longer.] And so I stripped the wallpaper with a razor blade, then I painted the walls until they are bright white, then I punched several holes into the walls to let some extra natural light in because I have always loved natural light and the truth is anything fluorescent aggravates my depression. Perhaps I would've felt better if my lovers' skeletons were not jaundice in color, but a greenish hue instead.

The Body Forest

I see caul straps hanging down from the trees and the
rain is rich with formaldehyde. I drag my knees through
the dirt. A vise grip with metal teeth comes out of my
skeletal womb and grabs hold of my thighs. [Yum this,
yum that,] the vise grip says and tears my legs into strip
steak. Famished, I save one slice for myself and toss the
rest to the side. Men climb down their house walls, secretly escaping their wives' bedrooms and bite my shoulders. They strip the tan off my bones. I am sickly pale. I
am a white-washed monster. I am a mayonnaise slick.
Men see me and try to lick butter out of my joints. It is
not sauce. I am bruised woman. I set fire to the caul. I
stick them in a metal pot and place them in the oven. I
cook the caul on high for three days. When the timer finally dings, I yank them out. They are gray ash with eyes
in the center. I skewer the bulbs and plant them beneath
gravestones. [I am curious if there will be some sort of

head, resurrected from beneath the dirt,] I say. Perhaps one with ash crowns of burnt caul. I strike the head with a metal hammer and push it back into the ground. Rocks roll over the top. Gone ash gone. I beat the head with a piece of leather skin. The hard heart meat of the clambering men leaves broken windows behind. Widows poke their heads out of the holes in the windows and cover their mouths with their hands weeping. [Hurt,] they cry. [Let the holy blasphemers rejoice! Let them rejoin their appendages and think of steak crackers. Oh, these open cracks in the floor. Let them keep bleeding. Let them make messes in the basement cracks. Who owns this attic spine? Who keeps crying around the windowpanes?] I nail the widows to a glass slab. I pull at the men's throats until their jelly abdomens snap. Gelatin cubes rattle on the floor. I step on them, grinding the fat into the floor. [Is that for us?] the widows ask. They lean forward, tearing their limbs off the nails by which they've been hammered to the floors of their flats. The widows drop their tongues onto the puddle. [Salt slick, pepper lick, slick our stomachs. If our stomachs do not make sense, lose them in the graveyard. If we find a man in the graveyard tear him with a knife. If the knife was a joke, find the joke inside our shoulders and shake it. Our shoulders are bone amalgamations. The bone matter pretended to be a heart, but it was not one. Instead the heart shook and made steaks. We eat those steaks with jars of our

uterus butter. Is there a uterus in the air? Could the air
be dead butter? Or are we lying to our spouses chomp-
ing dirt? The dirt flowed out of our ears and we turned
the ears into a monster made of deer parts and the deers
begged for steak even though we decided steak would no
longer fall into our stomachs. But sometimes the worst
stomachs are the best bowels and if we are lucky those
bowels gurgle wedding vows and if we make a vow to
the ceiling fan, we might as well keep that fan pressed
to our wrists because the wrists have faces of their own
and they keep bleeding tar slicks and if we can keep one
tar slick, just one, every day, we might be able to make a
child out of our sand wombs because with the tar slick,
our sand is fertile material, then we only need a fertility God(des) to blaspheme our breasts and if our breasts
were penile things, we would finally find those penile appendages made of sand for our sand wombs. Then the
meaty appendages could suddenly, finally, become erect
with meat, even before the priest rested the communion
wafers on our tongues,] the widows say.

In the Vinegar Realm

I bone the vinegar planes with my front teeth and my
ankle bones and even though one realm is not good for
me I cannot keep my neck on straight. [Once there was
a princess who had no head. But she was not a necro-
philiac beast. She had a heart. And it would beat promi-
nently while she stuck knives into her knees and thought
about the end of the princely life of the man she had been
promised to,] the vinegar planes say. They stagger in circles. They twitch and their skin sheds like snake scales,
like troll heads, like little goblin shoes thrown into a tree
and left to inherit the maggots. I do not listen to their
twitching. I have my bovine womb in one hand and my
vaginal monster in the other and both snap at the fingers
and leave bloody trails. [Menstruating, she is menstruating,] the vinegar planes shriek at me and blow foreheads
off their tabletops. But the blood goes everywhere. [This
half-breed spic can bite the ends of our balls,] the vin-

egar planes say. [They're all so loud—all of them.] I run in circles, tucking my spine into the back of my mouth. My eyes burn. My skin turns. I stare at a piece of roasted meat emerging from my knees. [Stop hurting me,] I say and cut up my stained ass. I whip the feces into a delicious soup. Thick brown cud appears on the top. Religious members stick their faces against the windows and twitch. [We are nourished entirely by yellowing books,] the religious members say. They chew with their mouths open. They eat book spines. Their teeth squeak on the covers. Lettuce sticks out of their eyes. [Green—our eyes are green. It's a sign of holiness,] the religious members say. They peel the leaves off the head of the lettuce and throw them on the floor. They stick their faces in hot oil. [Did you sacrifice your sad children to the bathroom mirrors,] the religious members ask. I shrug my shoulders. [We do,] they say. I shrug my hair. I shrug my neck. I shrug and I shrug and I shrug until my shrunken head drop onto my belly button. [Are you evil, quasi-evil, or possibly pseudo-evil,] the religious members shriek. I touch my rosary lungs just like Mother Superior taught me. [I keep counting the beads whenever I breathe but the prayers don't rattle correctly,] I say. The religious members lie across the vinegar planes and sigh until their lips turn blue. [We are broken, we have lost our faith,] they say. [We have lost the words our ancestors vomited into our hands inside their ancient texts. We think we used too much soap. Or at least, more than we wanted too. Of the sad masks, have you seen them? We painted them pale white, then added acetone. Now the masks say that they don't know us. They use their mouths on phallic things but their lips never go numb. It's terrible. All of it is. We keep forgetting how the children acted as our saviors but the iron that they needed had to have been born in a divine way.] The vinegar planes open and swallow the religious members. They bounce across the floors, then drop into an acid bath. [That is it,] the religious members say. [In a few minutes, demonic ooze will seep out of the walls, then that will be the end. We won't be able to tell our hands from our bottled innards.] I pat my throat confidently. I touch my sequined lungs. Black stretches of fabric wrap around my face, constricting my jaws. I choke. I vomit over the polymer material—it doesn't breathe—and all my regurgitation stinks of vinegar and peaches. [That is the end,] the religious members say. [Everything that was meant to happen did. We are alone in your face, acting out our temptations with just a rope and some steak knives.] The vinegar planes touch my ankles. They stroke my feet. They hum into the religious members' ears. [Do you want a beef loin,] they ask and stain the walls blue.

At the end I swallow the sleeping pills because they taste like old milk—sweet and chalky. [How do you know what it tastes like,] the walls ask as they shed their old plaster. They wriggle and writhe, then release several thick sheets of pungent cream. [It is all the same color, your pills and our cream,] the walls whisper. [Even when painted how can you tell the difference? What does that tell you about your anatomy?] The walls shut down, their moldings catching hold of the tiles and wrenching them up. [It means nothing. It means genetic laziness. Something, you, refused to explore the options. Because that is the easy way. Because the body shouldn't be manipulated as much as you manipulate it. But don't listen to us. Your body is like every other person. It wants to betray you. You'll see,] the walls say. They sag in their centers. I put my fingers between my front teeth and bite slowly. I wait to feel pain. I wait to feel anything. I want to be reassured that I am right. But my fingers are like butter. My teeth feel no resistance. My teeth slide through my fingers and the bite coats my face with old lard fat. [Pity,] I whisper. [I thought the glass could hold.] I climb over the wall parts. I knock the tiles over. I place the metal into my jaws and twitch. [Someone should have told the planet to stay still. But they let it go out on some wild orbit. Now we have to suffer through the skewed gravity. And a warped mirror. What looks like a shower of dust are really tiny skin fragments that I tore off of me with a long sheet of masking tape,] I say to the walls. I put my butter fingers in my mouth. I suckle lactation from under the nails. [I am a child again,] I whisper and curl up on the belly lap. I push my hands further into my belly. My elbows push out of my rectum. [Is this natural,] I ask. My eyes thicken. I yank gashes off the walls and arrange them over my face like scars. [Much better,] I say. [Now I am like you, like everyone. Only more physical.] I do not focus on anyone who stares. They touch the raised bumps and place the lines on their tongues like a strange communion. [I once saw a man who could die and come back to life as many times as he pleased. But he found a blood clot and he wanted help. So he let someone see him die and come back to life and they strung him up in a meat-locker until the following morning when he was turned into concrete.] [None of that is the problem. The problem is that you refuse to take a bite of our cream,] the walls say. They lick their lips in anticipation of my communion. They twist their mouths into many smaller pieces. [We thought you'd be using larger jaws,] the walls say as they open the door. The walls play with my ovaries. They grab the fertile pieces and bend them over their walled wrists. [Punishment,] the walls say and clap their vaulted beams together. I cannot keep the wrinkles straight. The wrinkles leave my head and fester, growing and becoming more lined. [Did you forget the lights again?] I ask and the walls lunge at me. I hold up a fire poker to defend myself. I threaten them with an open can of paint. [We're not worried about you keeping your hands on your head,] the walls say. [Just like we know you won't use the paint to hurt us. Think of our floorboard children, the little cousins tucked into the bed. All of them. Because they are your only true family,] the walls finish. The walls pour red fluid everywhere. The walls cringe and the walls cry. [Love us again,] the walls say. [We keep a half-dissolved man strung up by his wretched toes.] They point at the abandoned wooden pantry closet. But there is no man in there. If there is, he is just an assortment of raised wounds covering the hard parts around his neck.

Organ Meat is Killing Me

(My Spine)

My spine hisses in my ear. [I will eat you,] it whispers. My spine moves up and down my back, biting its own bone plates and sucking the marrow out. [Self-cannibalism,] my spine says, sticking its tips into my ear. I walk with my head down and my spine up. My spine bites everyone it meets. It grabs them with its iron-tipped nerves and drops them on their backs, breaking the columns. [I do not have any loyalty to my vertebral family,] my spine says. My spine watches me when I sleep. It slides out of my body and curls up beside me, twitching in time to my breathing. My spine pokes my ribs until the bones push out of my skin. I wear my skeleton on the outside. My spine insists on living inside my throat. I swallow and everything tastes like spinal fluid. [Would you stop thinking about the yellow,] my spine snaps. It thrashes around until my chest aches. I vomit vertebrae. Each bone strikes the floor and bounces away, leaving a trail of bone shards behind. My spine pushes me down and makes me follow the flakes. [Eat them,] my spine says and pushes my head against the ground. I eat the bones and they taste like my skin. My spine has made me eat my skin as well. It lifts my wrist to my mouth and hisses, [Take a big bite.] If I do not, my spine lashes me until my middle welts with bruises, so I dig my teeth into my arm and I do not like the way my skin tastes. I am strange meat. My spine salivates in my ear. [I want to devour you fully,] it says. [But then, if I digest everything, I won't have anything else to look forward to. I won't have a body to live in.] So the spine eats me slowly, stealing bites from my feet and elbows. My spine likes my mucus and my hard things. It crunches and grinds its column on me until its nourishment is a pulverized yellow. [Say you love yellow,] my spine says as it opens my mouth. My spine pushes kidney stones onto my tongue. [Now say it,] it hisses. [I love yellow,] I say. But my words are garbled. It sounds like, [Eh uhv elluh.] My spine cuts my tongue with a knife. [I am branding you,] it says. [So that way, when you die, I get first pick of your meat.] I cry in the shower while my spine soaps my meatiest parts clean. It cuts my flesh in perfect circles punctuated with its initials. [Isn't there anything else you can eat?] I ask and my spine screams. It sticks its nerves in my ear and bursts my ear drums. [There is nothing else,] my spine says. [I was created to devour you. I've been eating you muscle by muscle ever since you were a baby. Those growing pains in your back? They came from my biting. Your scoliosis isn't a spinal curvature birth defect; it is the parts of the back still left intact from my daily binges. I like to eat in a figure eight. I make S's because they are part of my name.] Sometimes I push the spine away. I hold a fork to its marrow, and I threaten its nerves with a knife. When I do this the spine punishes me. It wraps its cord around my throat and squeezes my neck until the room spins bright yellow and red. [Am I dying?] I ask and the spine releases me. [Not yet. There's still much more for me to eat,] it says. It bites the sides of my throat. My spine vomits the meat it eats into my stomach. I digest myself. My spine bites my abdominal walls. [The paradox of all the acidic ages. How does the body eat itself without eating itself,] it asks. Its vertebrae spread. I can see my stomach inside, churning acid walls, spine yellow.

(My Uterus)

My fat uterus snakes out of my mouth and chokes me with its trailing innards. [What sort of fertile thing are you,] my uterus asks and plugs up my nose. I blink and see red. My uterus pours red fluid over my face. It drowns me in the fluid. I cannot smell a thing. I fling my hands around and smack the uterus away. It slinks along the walls. It leaves blood stains everywhere. The bright red turns brown quickly. I wipe my fingers across it. I bite my nails off and spit them onto the floor. My fallopian tubes snake out of the bed. They wrap around my wrists and snap my delicate bones. I cry and my throat aches. [I will eat you,] my fallopian tubes say. I strike them with sharp things. I rake blades down their lengths. I cut my tongue and throw tiny pieces of flesh at my uterus. It hangs down from the ceiling. It swings back and forth. The mucus splatters my face. I wipe and my skin comes off. My uterus releases noxious gases into the atmosphere. It burns holes through the walls. It pushes me against the remaining spaces and screams in my ears. [Cut me out why don't you,] my uterus shouts and licks around my cheeks. I find a hammer beneath the bed. I hit my uterus in its head. Or the base of its neck. Or its vase-like center. I do not know the parts of a uterus. Before this, I only thought of my uterus as a slab of hollowed out meat. Now it quivers and clenches and moans my name in the dark. [Why did you give my contents up,] my uterus screams. [I did what I was sup-posed to. I supported the flesh. I housed it on my walls until it could spread its arms. But you scraped it out. You vacuumed it out. And now I am vacant again. I am not supposed to be alone.] I hate my uterus's voice. I slam my uterus against a vise and grip the roundest part of its body until the flesh shudders and melts. [I can bring myself back together again,] my uterus says and releases three entire walls from its entry hole. Rancid blood slicks my hands. I wipe them across a tolling bell. The metal rusts faster than I meant for it to. I clang the bell but the sound mutes. My uterus squeals. [I am a uterus pig. Look at my skin. Give me your bacon hide and your little pieces of skin folds and I will show you how fatty I can be. Where is the girl who took her ax against her parents' heads? She knew what she was doing when she swung it. Her uterus was forced open by her father's hands. That was why she kept on cutting him. Poor girl. She just wanted to get back what he had taken out,] my uterus says. It flops around the room. It touches the green flecks of paint and tears them down. Wallpaper sags from the ceiling. It droops down towards the floor. It curls in thick sheets. The wallpaper rolls down to the floor and rests at my feet. My uterus stares at the paper. [You are not the kind of girl I am supposed to throw out,] it says. [But you are also not the kind of girl I should ever cut up. But I want to. Because you remind me of an apple mouth. And I have been afraid of apple mouths for longer than I ever should have been.] My uterus swings its arms. It fastens its bag body around my head. Everything goes tight and dark. I scratch at my uterus. I collect the bloody skin beneath my nails. My uterus squeezes harder. It gasps and contracts. [You're just hurting yourself,] I say. [I'm hurting you,] it responds. I grab a bottle of bleach and pour it over my uterus. It goes flat. It turns sickly white. [I am dead,] my uterus says and becomes still.

(My Fallopian Tubes)

In the center of my stomach, my fallopian tubes weave around my internal organs and flex just enough to birth a baby made out of mucus and foam. [This is your child,] my tubes say and vomit. The mucus baby rolls around in my intestines. It catches a flap of my thin skin in its mouth and bites down hard. [You must let it teethe,] my fallopian tubes say as it spits out the rest of the foam. I strike my bowels against the floor. [Stop trying to ruin everything,] my tubes say. I throttle my fallopian tubes with both of my hands. I strangle the tubes until the flesh turns bright blue. [You cannot kill us,] my fallopian tubes say and split into several entities. The one with the greatest amount of menstrual fluid slaps against my face. [You are staining my cheeks with a ruddy ruby red hue,] I say and my tubes laugh. [You are acting like the dunce we always knew you were,] my tube says, slipping out of my hands. It bites me. I regurgitate ovarian cysts. The fetal monsters climb out of my gums and roll across my tongue, slicking the meat in my mouth with amniotic fluids. [It burns,] I say and the babies laugh. [You are our mother,] the babies say. They cling to the backs of my eyes, clawing at my whites until my optical guts hang out of my facial hollows. [I hate the way you taste,] I say and the amniotic things struggle to get past my jawbones. [Mandibular creations,] my fallopian tubes shriek. They wind around my knees and constrict the joints. I wipe my muscles free. [Stop trying to bite me,] I say and the reddest fallopian tube hisses. [Do you want to be blue,] the tube asks. [Because we can make that happen. If you want to suffocate we can make that happen, too. We have all the flesh needed to prick you until you bleed out on the floor. Stop making this difficult for yourself. All you have to do is sit back and let the children come at you with their butter knives raised in the air and ready to spread your soft yellow fat.] My fallopian tubes slide along the bottom of the walls. They eat the plaster off the foundation and open their black hole maws to show me the red fibers dripping inside. [Do you see anything you like,] my fallopian tubes ask, puking thick clots of blood onto the floor. I kick the bloody moisture away. [I see nothing that I like. Only things that make me want to vomit,] I say. My fallopian tubes grimace and bloat. [Bad girl,] they say. [Bad, bad girl. Why don't you get heavier with our mucus membranes? Do you suffer from a constipated throat? Do you build moats around your bowels so that the antibodies cannot get through?] I break my fallopian tubes. I use my hands and feet. I nail my tubes to the wooden floor and screw them into place. [You will never get free again,] I say and my tubes shrivel from lack of moisture. I bend at the waist. I flex my hips. More tubes slither out of me and join their sisters on the ground. [We are actually boys,] the tubes say. [We have an equal opportunity sexuality because we get bored with all the constant femininity. What would you have done otherwise? Be surrounded by wombs?] My fallopian tubes drip into a puddle. They slap their ends around. Their sharp tips break through the ground and draw the termites up and out. [Is that a new venereal disease?] I ask. My fallopian tubes gasp for air. [You don't even know what you're saying,] they say. [There is no sex disease. Everything comes from the skin. Externally. That is what they mean.] They lift their nailed ends to their broken openings.

(My Knees)

I used to bleed my knees onto the floor and hiss loudly at them. [You cannot hurt me,] I say while my knees drip marrow everywhere. I push the yellow fat away but it is worse than butter and oil. It clings to my skin and hisses loudly as well. I spread the yellow fat around my ears where it mingles with wax and hardens into a residue. [We resist room temperature changes,] my marrow says. My knees seize and snap. They buckle beneath my weight. [I am not the heaviest; there are many heavier than me,] I say. [Why are you breaking?] My knees jump out of my legs and scatter across the floor. [It is something to do,] they say and rub against my stomach until my navel foams mucus. White fluid spills onto the floor and slicks everything. [You have a twisted this and a twisted that. You have a twisted cyst and a twisted back,] my knees say. [But we know better than you do. All those twisted things are liars. You don't have anything worse than a crumbled spine. Like bacon bits. Meat crumbles. Stop complaining or else we will steal your thigh muscles.] My knees grapple with their bone plates. They hit the walls and open their hollow bones to let the ashes in. [Dead ancestors,] I ask. [No just pieces of dead skin,] my knees say. [Nothing dies in the body. It just dries up and goes away. Turns into ash. Or dust. Or whatever kind of powder air you want to call it. But it doesn't die. That would mean everything leaves entirely. And evidently, as is seen in funerals, there is always a little bit of something left behind.] I bind my wrists in razor wire. The metal pushes into my skin and chops my arms into several smaller pieces. [You are only adding to my army,] my knees say. [Now arrange your back so that I can have it as well,] it says. I bend over as far as I can and I bite my knees. They squeal like pigs. [We are not porcine products,] my knees say. [Stop hurting us,] they bleed. My knees lose their fat drippings. [We've gone arthritic in the span of a few minutes,] my knees scream as they beat against the underside of my face. I rub my stomach. It gurgles against my open palm. [Feed me,] my stomach says. I am not willing to kill anything and so I grab my knees and hammer their bone plates until the bone is spread into two large halves. [I am hungry,] I say and swallow the slices of knees. They kick around inside my throat. My stomach latches onto the marrow and yanks it down into the gurgling acid. It shrieks and sucks the marrow out of the knee bones until the acid bubbles and my abdomen distends. [This is painful,] I say. My broken knees crawl out of my pelvis. [It is worse for us,] they say. [You stole our calloused bruises away. You took the cushioned air pockets. You left us with acrid calcium. What can we even do with that? Nothing. We are brittle now. We are pockmarked with holes. Like a cheese left for the maggots to eat. You won't be able to stand up on us because we will shatter into a million tiny pieces that you'll never be able to piece back together, even with the help of super glue.] My knees blow their last fat pockets out. They touch my skin. They breathe loudly and split again. [We'll miss you,] my knees say as they slink into the ruined closet. They close the door behind them. They rattle around in the dark. [Be careful. There are blades down there,] I shout and an ax falls upon their bones. I listen to the crushed calcium roll. Thin mucus puddles seep out from beneath the closet door. I guide the puddles into my open hand. I stick my tongue into the fluid. [Too salty,] I say as I spit the mucus back towards the closet.

(My Skin)

If my skin unravels from my bleached white bones and the prancing ligaments bend and whirl from my tendons, I will be nothing more than a pale bone frame coated in steak bits, made to drop off the asbestos-hued asylum walls. [What we do is simply bite your face,] my skin says and takes a chunk out of my leg. I am gaping and I am destroyed as my skin bite threatens to deceive me. Everything born of my flesh quakes and turns away until the gelatinous membranes form across the shocked expanse of my face. But what am I if I am not the little girl once torn to pieces before the organ wolves and their immortal vertebrae? [Give us the red red, the haunting red, the very reddest red,] the wolves sing floating on the stiff planks of their backs, while my skin things graze upon their tongues, blowing their tastebuds to pieces. And the muscle. How it drops apart so quickly in the expanse of one month of lunar cycles and menstruation clots. [We will eat the black tar blood off your faces,] my skin says and screams until my body drains of all the intestinal fluids. [Give us this, give us that, until your intestines find a crack in abdominal walls they can fit through without loosening their endless bowels,] says my endless skin. My musculature goes bald and singes my skin. [I am bloody and muddy,] I say and my skin slithers its serpentine lengths around my fingers. It splits the joints into several parts. [Stop hurting me,] I say and my skin sticks its bulk down my throat. Or is it the skin's throat? I cannot tell anymore as my skin winds into me, then slithers out again, coated in brown waste and green bile. [These products are better than your exterior,] my skin says shaking off the muck. I bite my skin. I tear through it with my teeth and hiss until my jaws snap. [You cannot eat me,] my skin says and jumps off my bones. It does not go far. My skin leaves and flops to the floor. [Sickening,] I say, lifting the skin with a wooden stick. It clings to the dry twig. [You have left me to fend for your own bowels,] my skin says. My skin sags and drips down again. I leave it to sink into the cracks between the floorboards. [You are just a flesh mound,] I say and the bowels adjust to fit inside my palms. I break my shins. I follow a flashing red light into the basement corridor. A man pauses just outside the closet door. [Are you missing your skin,] he asks. [Don't be alarmed. It isn't a rare story. And it's not as if I woke up in a tube filled of ice inside a back alley,] I say. The man cuts his tongue off. He throws the muscle at my face. [I've never seen anything like you before,] he says and hisses. My skin crawls up his legs. [Let's kill him,] it says strangling the man. My skin takes his flesh off. It wraps the new flesh around its sagging muscle and stands tall. [Now I can devour you without swallowing,] it says. I force a smile and my skin strikes at my throat. It bites my jaw bones. It leaves large wounds across my neck. [I want you to stop hurting me,] I say and splash the skin with bleach. Its thick muscle tones burn. The bleach dribbles through the pores. It eats the pigmentation up. White splotches spread. [This is how the red things were turned away,] I say. My skin curls up. It coils in the bleach basin. [No more,] it moans and its colors fade.

(My Intestines)

My intestines spindle out of me and moan about facial expressions that I make. It complains that my stomach acid is made up of diluted oil. [If you eat us, you will die. But if we bite you, then you will turn to dust,] my intestines say knocking me onto an operating table covered with IVs. I bite the needles that it dangles over me. I tear at the tubes with my hands. [I am disgusted by your bloated face, you digestive thing,] I say. I leave my flesh, then drop back into it. [You are sick,] my intestines say winding around me. [Snake intestines. Piece of garbage intestines,] I spit. I leave my entrails hanging from my stomach for the cannibal angels to devour with their front teeth. [Do you hear the bleating on the ceiling,] my intestines ask. The angels I prayed for torture my bowels with their roots. My intestines shriek and dig into my foot while I hobble on my stilted ankles. [Dirty meat things,] the cannibal angels sing and tap my hands with their metal tipped nails. Loops of my intestines drip out of their mouths. My intestines break the angel jaws and strike their joints with their iron claws. [You are stronger than we fantasized,] my intestine says tearing the angels' wings into halves. The angels bang around on the ground unable to fly. They grapple with their fingernails and try to fly until their buttocks hover just barely above the floor. [This is not work, let us crawl,] the angels say and shift into a cubbyhole. They tuck their spines into a tiny corner groove. [It is better to be the teeth than the meat,] my intestines say triumphantly as they lift wooden planks the digestive way. For the first time, I touch my feet. To break the meat I use a hammer and a pair of rusted nails. My intestines stretch out on the wood floorboards and their flesh gets everywhere. [The black parts are the shit stains,] I whisper to my intestines as they moan in disgust. When I am not looking, my intestines hit my shoulders. My intestines bang against the walls until plaster drops down in thick sheets. [By might or by nothing, the walls stay standing, how is that,] the intestines laugh. They suck the plaster down their throats and gasp. [And now we are heavy with raw materials,] my intestines say. My intestines tear the ground in two, whirling around their plaster hoses. [Do you do or do you not do,] my intestines ask dropping their guts down a flight of rusted metal stairs. [The rust and the must and the nothing,] my intestines say shifting around in my throat. They grapple with my tonsils and pretend to build a moat of my rib bones around my cardiac holes.

[This vein is not a man but a doll thing,] my intestines say. They tap their hands against my thighs. They grab the walls and lick the wood. [We do not want splinters,] my intestines say. They vomit angel wings and hiss. [No more vomit,] they shriek. My intestines grumble with wet gut movements. They cringe and bite my fists with their tiny incisor teeth. [Let us call to the belfry bowels,] my intestines say. [Or let us be better than we were when we began this hunger sacrifice.] My intestines slink into the bedroom and crawl over the far wall. They lap the paint up. [So we cry,] they say and they flop onto my bed. They turn to dust. Their sagging flesh becomes heavy cold fat. My intestines swipe the pillowcases and push artificial feathers up their tubes. The nylon irritates their skin. Their flesh turns into deep blisters infected by several green bacterial cultures. The cannibal angel intestines move into the sheets. They eat the fabric pieces. [Let us sob together as one,] they say and remove the cannibal angels from the attic crawlspaces. [So we moan,] the intestines say in unison.

(My Kidneys)

If I allow these kidney beasts to get a taste of meat, they will turn into cannibal goblins groping at gaping innards while screaming profanities about prosthetic dolls and obese genitals. I must keep the pork-chops away from my stomach but my kidneys push against my abdomen demanding to be fed. They writhe around in my skin, struggling to break free from my musculature. [You have to stop trying to bite me; everything else has already bitten me,] I say as my kidneys wriggle out of my navels and onto the counter-top. My kidneys yank at my chest. They grab meat from marinated dishes and push the protein into their porous flesh. Their deep red flesh pustules pulse. I close my eyes. I push the kidneys back in. They twist in my hands and bite my fingers. [You really are delicious,] my kidneys say. They vomit the pork-chops from yesterday out and bite my hands again. I lose part of my wrists. I grab at the split blood vessels and cry. My kidneys sputter. [It burns,] I say. [It tastes so sweet,] they respond. They latch onto the broken vessels and draw the blood in. I push the kidneys back but they bite into my skin and cling. [Let me go,] I say as my kidneys dart up my arms. They tear the muscle and throw it to the floor. [This is a feeding frenzy,] my kidneys say. [Look at how ravenous our mouths are.] I hit the organ meat with my heavy bones and the kidneys moan. [Do not treat us like we are so weak,] my kidneys say. [We want to break you into pieces.] [You'll just digest yourself,] I say. My kidneys laugh. They dart through the cabinets and drink cleaning solvents until their scarlet flesh turns bright gray. [We are ruined,] they say. They peel the splattered portions off and scream. I break my kidneys between my hands. I squeeze until the muscles burst and kidney juice flows out from between my fingers. The juice drips onto the floor. [You are as bad as we used to be,] the juice says. The juice flows over my feet and eats through my skin. [Why are you reducing me?] I ask. The juice trickles up my leg and eats through the bone marrow. [Go to the street,] my kidneys say. I break through the window. The window shatters and glass tears through my flesh. [So much pain,] my kidneys whisper into my ears. It burns through my cheeks. It tears through the muscle. I cringe and scratch frantically, dislodging the clotted kidney chunks. [This is wrong,] I say. My kidneys howl. Their meat flows into the street, collecting in the gutters and slicking the curbs. [Do you see?] I ask. [I see food,] my kidneys say. The juice sloshes over the parked cars, submerging them in bile. My kidneys tear through basements, catching housewives as they do their laundry, ruining men's eyes as they peer into heated boilers. [You have gone wild,] I say. My kidneys spin in circles. They extend their droplets and sink to every lawn they touch. [What did you expect,] my kidneys ask. [We got a taste of meat and had to have more. Do not deny us. We'll eat your eyes out.] My kidneys rip through my shins. Their juice coats my throat and burns through the ligaments. [Do we turn you into a piece of skin later? A fat slick? An oil barrel? We don't even know how we tore ourselves out of you,] my kidneys say. The juice slathers and lathers and blathers around my legs. I throw salt down. I add flour. I mix warm water into a bowl of sour yeast. I dry the juice up. I make it into a kidney pudding. It is surprisingly delicious.

(My Offal)

My organ meat is killing me. It moves slowly through my bowels and flays each fleshy hallway with a single bone spine that stretches past the reach of its joints. [Skin is the same as meat which is the greatest protein ever held in the mouth,] my organ meat says. I churn the organ meat in a heavy aluminum tub. [May I keep the fatty glands,] my organ meat asks. It falls to its fake knees and twitches until the sinew loosens. [The more tender, the better,] my organ meat says. My organ meat pickles nicely and keeps in the refrigerator for several hundred years while I lie in the empty boiler, learning how to separate my meat from my bones. [This is too much,] I say and the boiler breaks around my head. I stretch and the head of the boiler snaps. The boiler rolls across the floor. It flattens my organ meat. It smoothes the flesh into a patty form, then a steak. [We are wrong,] my organ meat says. It clings to the boiler sides and sucks the aluminum down. The organ meat strips the boiler down to sheet metal and pats its iron-filled stomachs. [Much better,] my organ meat says. The organ meat pushes me onto a table and inserts needles into my skin. [Where does this lead to,] I ask. [To us,] my organ meat says as it pushes tiny kernels of flesh into its vials. My veins fill with the meat. My arms clot. I struggle to keep the meat in but my arms can only take so much pressure pushing up from the vessels. [It aches,] I say and the meat comes up from my pores. I suffer black and blues of the darkest reds. Blood flows through my skin. It slicks my face with moisture. I cross my eyes. I keep my arms behind my back and my organ meat seasons my stomach with pepper and onions. [Shall we eat,] it asks as I lean forward in the first stages of a fatal disease. [This infection began in my throat,] I say. It burns me. Red cysts run up and down the inside of my neck. I swallow needles to pop the blisters. Green bile dribbles out of the cysts and leaves a sour taste in my mouth. [Is there any cure?] I ask. My organ meat twitches knowingly, but it tells me nothing. It braids its bacon meat. It pulls the thin skin sinew off its limb-like parts and wraps them around its head portion. [There is no cure because we do not believe in one that is not death,] my organ meat says. The organ meat seizes up around my chest. It breaks my bones. It powders the enamel and leaves the calcium in several small yellow pieces. [Do not even begin to think about the stomach twists,] it whispers and licks the sides of my face. It rakes my cheeks off. I stick alcohol-soaked swabs into the raw skin and cut the bacteria off. [We are dying,] the bacterial cultures say. They sizzle and fizzle. The cultures drop from my skin. I step on them. My organ meat rubs itself over the bacteria and whimpers prayers. [Let us pray to the bacteria, how it fidgets against our bone structures and sobs for our special wills,] my organ meat says. My organ meat cuts itself with rusted scissors. It throws the slabs at my chest. [I do not want to touch you,] I say. My organ meat covers my hands. It piles up on the ceiling and drips down slowly, striking my forehead with each individual droplet. The droplets burn and I cover my face with my hands. [Broken girl,] my organ meat says. I sink into a chlorine pool and soak my meat wounds.

(All of Me)

Porcine products burst out of me and they reek of bacon. My organ meat jumps around inside of me, trying to grab at the ligaments. [We are starving,] my limbs say and stuff the pork products down my throat. [I am a slaughtered pig piece. I am a woman made out of fried pig ears. Hear me cry,] I bellow. [Or hear me bleed out on the dirt floor made just to catch the fluids in my blood,] I whimper, dripping plasma remnants. I cook pieces of skin sans the body glove of pork intestines pulled above the shoulder planks. [Let us bow our heads in silence,] I pray. I wear a meat hook as a necklace and my body parts try to bathe me in yellow fat but I am unwilling to have the slick fluid touch my skin. [You will not marinate me,] I say and my body parts rumble. My guts turn in circles until I vomit on the floor. [Lovely pieces of bacon guts,] my guts say. They eat it themselves without think-ing. [Pork for my mother, pork piece, pork beast, pork from inside the gutter,] I say as I swing from the curved metal hook ends jutting out of my wrist bones. Like a piece of meat, I drop into a refrigerator. The meat pieces flutter in the cool breeze. They grab my hands. They bite my fingers off. [We are hungry for your bacon bits,] they say and tear at my ankles while I glue my lashes shut for safekeeping. Everyone tries to bite me, everyone always has. I ooze steaks and chops and rib things. I am a piece of flesh gone missing, then found again on the oiled slab, seasoned around the fat sides, while I hope for a saintly death and a more anatomical departure. [You get nothing,] my body parts say. [We won't let ourselves be turned into dust because of your squeamishness.] They leap onto my tongue and tear my taste buds out. I flap my tongue muscle around. I touch the tip to my nose. My lungs die down. They cringe and flip. They implode. [Will you treat us like poultry breasts,] my lungs ask, gagging for the last bit of air in my system. They fade to gray before I can answer. But I will treat them kindly. I will use them like nylon safety ropes when I climb sev-enteen walls just to find a ceiling that I can use the blood vessels in. They don't remember what it feels like to carry the liquid things inside of me. They tucked their frayed ends into the tubes and hoped for the best. [If there are holes, the pork will know,] I say and my lungs inflate slightly. Then they flatten and my lungs might as well be an appendix. They are just as useful, lying against the muscles with their hollows left empty. [At least fill your parts with stones,] I shout and we both tremble slightly. [I have gone crazy,] I say and the pork products push out of my eyes. I wipe my face and the porcine fat covers everything. [This is too strong of a protein,] I say. [It is a fat source] my tongue corrects me. [Or a fat source. It is too strong and fat for anything. And I cannot abide by its stench,] I say. The pork eats my legs. I locate a tiny nostril gland in the center of its fake face. [You are not pork, you are just plaster. You cannot eat me,] I say as my bowels move. They rock inside my throat until I vomit into a bottle filled with vodka. [Now my waste is clean, disinfected,] I say. I splash the vodka into a cup filled with fresh pork shavings. [It is just as fresh as the pork that came out of my mouth,] I say as I sip the drink. I sputter; the pork tasted disgusting. A motor oil flavor stains my lips. I wipe the fluid off with a washcloth made of pumice stones and powdered quartz. I stick my head into a bathroom sink lacquered with grease. My bowels move across my cheeks. [Stop trying to bleed us,] they scream. The pork pieces bend against my chest. I feed them from a bladder trough. That seems to satisfy them.

(My Body)

My body cremates me and every blow torch is just another ligament I thought I knew. [This is it, this is the end,] I say, sifting through my powdered remains. [The exhaustion has come for me.] I fold my hands behind my head and lie across the cold body of a rusted radiator. [Do not fall apart,] I say to the steam vents. The radiator stands tall. It keeps its roots tucked into the walls. I lick the metal until my tongue falls out. [I am clean,] I whisper. But I am not clean. I am a mess. And I cannot pull the bread of my body out of my bowels. I vomit fluid. I shit gas. Saran-wrapped red meat products rub against my breasts until my nipples ache. [I do not want any part of you,] I say and break the men into thirds. No, I divide them in quarters, then I steal three-fourths of the body parts to store in my favorite cauldron oven. [I can cook anything in the matter of only a few minutes,] I say with pride. I fall to my knees and pray to the toilet gods. [There are gods in every nook and cranny,] I say while prying a God of the fingernails out of my knuckles where he got lost while going to a meal in my subterranean areas. My eyes are heavy. They might as well fall out of my face while I try to screw the whites into my pink hollows. [Look. This is not what I wanted,] I say and my eyes flatten. They run across my hands and become a piece of paper. [But you are lined,] I scream. [How can I have full creative control?] I ask. The already cremated parts of me drop out of my nose. They come out in every drip and in every tear that I shed. I collect the gray fluid on a paper towel and hang it up to dry in front of the kitchen window. [There might be a pattern that is important for me to see,] I say as I try to read the runoff. But the colors squash and squiggle. I cannot see any words. [The pattern might be a symbol,] the pork says returning from its bout with hoof in mouth disease. The meat is tainted. The organs make cakes out of my ash meat. [It is just dust; it has no secret meaning,] I scream. The organs flavor the dust with salt and pepper. They sear it in an oiled pan until a black crust forms around the outside. [Isn't it better to be golden brown outside than to be burned?] I ask and the organs stare at me dumbfounded. They flip the cakes once and stack them up on their shoulders. [You're cute,] the organs say. [But you were cremated several years ago. Stop trying to act like your body parts are still together. No one wants to hear it. You muscles have burned. Your face is burned. Your teeth are burned. Everything is burned. So you really don't have a place here.] The organs push me into a food processor. The organs turn the speed up to high and whip my bowels into a frothy cream. [Let us mourn the great creamy passing,] the organs say as they bleed from their thin exteriors. [I didn't have enough iron supplements when I had you,] I say. [I am so sorry that I neglected you. And now look at you; you can't retain any vitamins without me. But I've been cremated, and now you've blended me. You can't do anything without me. You don't even have a mouth to push food into. I will probably just go to waste.] The organs cringe at my truth. The organs run in circles. The organs run scissors in half-moon shapes around their eyes and fold the skin down. [You are a bitter piece of skin anyway,] the organs say. [We will make a mouth another way,] they proclaim. They fit a hanger into the space between my thighs. The organs crack their bony residue. [Close your eyes and hope,] the organs say, rinsing the slick fluid off. I hold my eyes closed. The organs yank the tops of their meat off. My burned muscle crumbles in their hands. [Better,] they sob as they take their places in the stew pot.

(My Spleen)

Body mold seeps out of my spleen and coats my innards in green gook. [I am sick,] I moan and the pain feels like a ruptured ovarian cyst. I stick needles into my pus-filled mounds. [Are you trying to eat me?] I ask my spleen. It bites my intestines and ruins my digestive tract. [Your acid will eat you so I don't have to,] my spleen says. The mold burns a hole through my stomach. I reach into the gap and scrape out several pounds of crusted spores. [Stop growing,] I say and wipe bleach around the hole. The mold colonies squirm around my fingers. I cut their roots off with a rusted pair of scissors. The mold spores bite the blades off. They shake the metal around and scrape the mercury beads on the points. I squeeze the mold spores until the green juice flows out from between my fingers. [Stop ruining my moldy children,] my spleen says waving its dismembered hand around in the air until the jointed fingers drop away from the palms. I gather the little meat fingers against my neck and toss them into a food processor. [If you're hungry, then you should eat the meat you've been producing,] I say. My spleen grumbles. It does not like to be corrected. My spleen pokes against the inside of my stomach. It leaves long furrows across my abdomen. I fill the spaces with wet concrete and stand in front of a blow-dryer until the mixture hardens into steel. [The mold will eat you from the inside,] my spleen shouts. [Don't you know any better than to bite the spleen that filters you?] [You don't filter me,] I say. [Just the urinary portions.] The spleen jumps onto my shoulders and latches onto my neck. It pulls my skin until I bruise. [Same thing,] the spleen shrieks, grabbing my ears. [It is all the same thing! How did you think the urine was separate from the shit or the lubricant? There are pores in there. They are joined. Siamese organs. Stop judging the body processes. I cannot stand the curves of your face,] it screams. My spleen slides down my arms. I knock the creature to the floor. [Where did all the mold come from?] I ask, nailing my spleen's center to a vinegar-rubbed cutting board. My spleen strains against the nail.

It wriggles and turns in circles, lacquering the cutting board with its reddish bile. [From outside the window,] my spleen grunts, pushing up against the nail. The nail does not move. My spleen folds its body around the slick body and thumps. [What does the mold want?] I ask. My spleen hisses and vomits onto the counter. [It wants to eat you. What else does any organism—fungus, mold— want? We only support you until you're fat enough to feed us,] my spleen says pressing harder against the nail in its center. The nail wobbles slightly. Sensing the nail's weakness, my spleen kicks the nail, destroying the cutting board in the process. [Leave the wood alone, it did nothing to hurt you,] I say and stick a fork through my spleen. I chop my spleen into pieces. The mold spores get in my eyes. My eyes sting. I stick wet paper towels against my face. Mold soaks into the paper and stains the pulp fibers bright green. [What are you?] I ask. The mold spores scream in unison and bite my retinas. [We are eggs gone wrong,] they say. [What do you get when you crack open a rotten egg? Us.] The mold spores giggle. They rock back and forth on my lashes, turning my head from side to side. My spleen sings in delight, [If we can turn your meat on end, then we can all get a much better serving.] I scour my arms with embalming scrub. I make mold balls seasoned with spleen meat. I won't be dry cured.

(My Breasts)

My breasts dress their fat with oil and vinegar, followed by a pinch of salt. I wake up in the morning and smell a fresh garden salad. Salad dressing slicks my chest and my hands slide across my abdomen. I spit up onions. [What have you done?] I ask and my breasts giggle. They lurch around on my chest until my pectoral muscles ache. [We were just waiting to get eaten,] they say. [You aren't meat. You are just fat glands,] I say. [That's the point. We are used for food production. Why are you keeping us from our true purpose? We just want to be used for the greater good,] the breasts say. [If someone eats you, it will hurt. You'll get sucked until you develop sores. Or you'll be flayed into steaks and once that's done, you'll be gone. You can't be brought back from the dead or the digested. Otherwise, I might as well sew silicon spatulas to my chest,] I say. The breasts fidget. They drip down to my belly. My chest muscles spread. I pat them with rubbing alcohol to keep any infections from spreading. [You're causing scarring,] I say. Again, the breasts laugh at me. They prick the tumors between my thighs. [What are those blisters,] they ask. [Scar tissue. The kind you made,] I say. [We were never that low,] the breasts say. They lift up forks and knives. I wrap sheets around my chest to keep the rest of the skin in place. My breasts bite through the bedding. [Stop trying to get dressed. We need to confer with a cookbook about what kind of cooking technique would be best for us. What do you think about barbecue,] they say. My breasts leap at the wall. I yank them back. My shoulders ache from the constant movement. I rotate my bones and my breasts moan softly, then swell. [We're retaining water,] they say. [Water or milk,] I ask. [Who said we were pregnant,] they say. [You were the ones mumbling about the greater good and the necessity of cooking for strangers. So why is milk production out of the question,] I ask. My breasts sigh. They tear through the sheets and leave ragged holes around their swells. [We aren't cows. What did you think? That we would just let rubber hoses latch onto our nipples so you can suck us night and day? We want the feeding process to be over and done with. Quick and easy. Because it's better for everyone,] my breasts sigh. My breasts come off my chest and run laps around the room. [You need to sweep, this place is a mess] they say, pausing in the corner nearest the closet. [I keep the door blocked with books and clothing, just in case someone wants to come in,] I explain. The breasts leap into the pile and push the hardest stuff away. [What do you think you're doing?] I ask, climbing off my bed. The breasts jump out the door. [We want to see the world. If we're not going to feed anyone, then we should be allowed to travel,] they say. My breasts scratch the walls on their way out. They sign the plaster: THE BREASTS. My breasts dart around the corner. I follow them into the basement. They roll down the wooden stairs and land on the bleach board at the back of the basement. They sort through the half-empty bottles, mixing some contents in plastic bins. [It is time for surgery,] my breasts say. They bow, giggling. They scrape their undersides against the uneven table. My breasts leap into the tub. Bluish liquid suds around the external skin. I cross myself like they taught me in Sunday school. My breasts bleed and sink into the mixture. [We're much cleaner now,] they say as they fall apart.

(My Body, Deux)

My body feeds me pills made out of dried crushed dead babies. [For your sexuality,] it says. [That's irony. Dead babies are so that I can keep ovulating,] I say. My body is not amused. It stabs me with a needle and I bleed slowly, dripping drop by drop, while my musculature cringes and bloats with steroid water. [Stop injecting me with fluids,] I say. My body grinds up my pills with salt water. It sticks the powdered fluid into a syringe. I snap the needle with my teeth. My body breaks the vial against my head and pours the fluid over my eyes and into my mouth. [You are blessed with a dead infant,] my body snickers while sticking its tongue out. I wipe the water from my eyes. The dead baby powder burns my throat. [Is it really filled with dried amniotic fluid and belly button curd?] I ask. My body shrugs. [It depends on what you believe,] my body says, lying down on the kitchen floor. It stretches out on the cold tile and stares up at the ceiling. My tongue turns blue. I stick my tongue out and touch the tip to my nose to see the color. My eyes cross. [I think my throat is burning,] I say. My body sits up. [You worry too much. Just relax,] my body says. My body lies down again. Saliva bubbles out of its mouth. The fluid wets the floor. I stick my hands into my mouth. [It's raining outside,] I say and listen to the droplets striking the windowpane. My body turns onto its side. [Stop worrying. Are you that afraid that the water will get in,] my body asks. I wipe my eyes with a wet towel. [Where did you get those pills from?] I ask. [I have to know.] My body curves upward, then flattens out. [We got it from another country. Or maybe we dug it up from the ocean. What do you care,] my body says. My abdomen trembles. I place my hands against the muscles and feel an egg drop out of my fallopian tubes. The egg pushes against the muscular walls and bleeds out. I push paper towels against my legs to catch the blood. [I'm sick,] I say and my body grinds its teeth together. [Stop worrying. This is all normal,] my body says. [I know ovulation is normal. But not this much. There's not supposed to be this much pain. I feel like my cysts are breaking,] I say. Unperturbed, my body curves into an S-shape. I lean forward to get its attention. I rock back and forth against the counter, pressing my abdomen down on the cool formica. [It hurts,] I say. My stomach burns. Another egg drops and pushes up against the first. [Your pills are killing me,] I say and my body stands up. [Stop being so dramatic. You're being a wimp. Have you ever felt the eggs drop before,] my body asks. [They were always scrambled,] I say, hoping that I was right. Three more eggs drop down at the same time. The pain is so severe that I vomit. Blue fluid runs off my tongue and flows onto the floor. It smells like digestive fluids, so I'm guessing that it is stomach bile. I push paper towels into my mouth to block the vomit from rising again. [You're hurting me,] I say. The eggs inside me pop. I drop to my knees and huddle in fetal position. [I'm dying,] I say. [I'm sure of it]. My body pours vinegar over my head. [This will help stop any bacterial growths,] my body says. It finishes the bottle and throws it across the floor. The eggs claw out of my uterus. They push out of my skin, digging through the flesh until a thin tunnel forms. They pop out, scramble across the floorboards and disappear into the wall cracks. The burning becomes worse. [Is it like being stuck with a fork,] my body asks. [No! It is like a twisting knife blade after a few minutes heating on top of a hot stove,] I say. My body laughs. It crushes the rest of the pills in its hands. [Snort, this will heal you,] my body says as it rubs the white powder across my nose.

(My Offal, Deux)

My organ meat builds heavy skyscrapers against me in my gut. The steel and glass push up to my throat and my tongue foams against the green and blue windows. [There is an entire landscape inside,] my organ meat sighs when I complain. It oozes down the glass sides. It mingles with the concrete foundations and slicks the metal bars. [Don't you think that the entire thing is lovely,] my organ meat asks. It jumps up my chest and pounds against my bone structure. [Leave my ribs alone,] I say as I smack the organ meat away. The organ meat foams in my mouth and covers my teeth. I spit the meat out. [I do not want any of your protein in my lungs,] I say swallowing a cup of bleach. First the organ meat turns bright yellow then it fades to white. [This is suicide,] it screams. [This is the worst sort of murder. Bleach? Really? You would scour us with bleach until we are dead? What is the matter with your taste buds that you would voluntarily drink such terrible things to destroy us?] I scrape the organ meat out of me with a hanger. It lies limply across the wire arm. [Stop. We are seeking refuge from this abuse. Asylum. Give us asylum,] my organ meat pleads to no one in particular. [I don't recognize asylum,] I say. I inject the organ meat with a syringe of chlorophyll. [We'll see what you look like when you turn green,] I say and stand back. My organ meat pickles. Its skin rises up until my organ meat huddles beneath itself.

Then the green slowly starts to show. At first it comes in spores and little blisters, popping up sporadically, while the organ meat claws its wrists and whimpers. [You have to stop. This is torture,] my organ meat says. [We have skyscraper constructions to complete. We have towers and bridges to build.] My organ meat reeks of rotten sinew. I pour milk over its body and my organ meat settles on the floor. Unattended, the skyscrapers within me fall over. Glass windows shatter. I choke the shards up. My throat burns. [We told you,] my organ meat says. [We told you that the towers would fall over. They can't be dependent on your skeletal structure.] [Of course they can. They are in my bowels. I can shit them out if I want to and leave them clinging to my rectal things. So why shouldn't I let them fall when you finally pull them away,] I say. The organ meat hisses. It throws feces at my face. [Add this to your organic structures,] my organ meat says, shoving shit down my throat. [We don't want to be a part of your circulatory skyscrapers anyways.] My organ meat slithers out of my slashed wrists. Green tendrils cover my nails. I crack my bones and pour the marrow onto my organ meat. The organ meat tilts itself upwards and ingests the liquid fat. [How did it come to be that we never realized how delightful we taste on an extended palate,] the meat sighs. It grabs my ankles and wrenches the bones up towards my shoulders. [Is there anything else stuck inside you,] my organ meat asks. It licks my legs and tears through my soft skin. [I do not want to go through life missing muscles,] I say. I season the organ meat with sea salt and roll it out on a plastic sheet. [Death to you,] I say. The organ meat flutters under my kneading. It leaks brown fluids. [But we are made out of you,] the organ meat says. It grasps my knees and rubs against my skin. [Do not eat us,] my organ meat purrs. [Do not reduce us down into a broth made for your cannibalistic tendencies.] The organ meat blows against my elbows. My bones inflate. [Time for the oven,] I say. I rake the organ meat over a bed of hot coals.

(My Offal, Trois)

I bake my organ meat at high temperatures. The yellow fat renders out and wets the floor. [Too dry,] my organ meat says. It flops around in the pan and reaches up to rattle the heat lamps until they break. The glass catches in the muscles and textures its skin. [We are mutilated,] the organ meat wails. I open the oven and cut the meat loaves with a heavy butcher knife. The meat cleaves into two halves. Tiny blue worms squirm through the muscle. I scoop the worms out. They bite my fingers. They draw my blood out. It pools up in my palms. I push the worms together and coat them with stale bread crumbs. I form a fritter and drop the breaded patty into a frying pan filled with hot oil. [We're sizzling,] the worms scream. They splatter in the oil. Oil droplets strike my cheeks. Blisters rise up on my face and turn bright brown. [This is painful,] the worms say. They cover my hands and drill through my palms until I can see through the holes to the floorboards. [Hallelujah,] the organ meat says. [Freed of those parasites, we are much better than before.] The worms squirm across my meat and lick splinters out of my bones. [This is what we do,] the worms say. I rip the organ meat over my head. I cut it and the worms into many tiny pieces. I shove them down the garbage disposal and grind it into a bloody chum. [Decorate us,] the meat worms say, coming back up the sewage pipes. They eat the silver in the solder. They vomit steel. I throw broken crystals at their tiny faces and stitch my fingers together. The crystals never seemed to work anyways. [Stop praying,] the organ meat pleads. The worms eat the tiny silverfish and belch. I close my eyes. I wag my spinal column until its bones threaten to drop off. [I am in much too much pain,] I say. The meat worms giggle in delight. They latch onto my nails. [We can teach you a thing or two about aesthetic preparation,] they say. The worms drill through my bones. They chew my skin and vomit the meat up. I wipe my eyes with thick pieces of steel wool and wait for their meat consumption assault to stop. [I am not a food source,] I say. The meat worms open their circular mouths. [What do we care,] they ask. [Do you not want us to put the crystals on your face? They are magical.] They douse my shoulders with glue.

The broken crystals drop out of the ceiling and stick to my skin. They glitter with bright red, greens and blues. The clear crystals reflect the ceiling light. They refract the light and a rainbow comes out of my skin. [I do not like how the spectrum burns,] I say. My spinal cord frays from all my scurrying. The column comes apart inside my back and vertebrae steadily drop out, striking the floor and shattering. [We can braise those bones to get the marrow out later,] the meat worms say. They touch my face gently. They steal raw vertebrae from me and push the meat into their mouths. The meat worms suck the fatty lard out. [Now for the crystals,] they laugh and lick across my cheeks until the skin comes off. The crystals dangle from their overhanging lips. They sparkle. They glitter. They set off the black of the meat worms' eyes. [Join us in the crystal mines,] the meat worms say. They spit the precious gems up and push the crystals into the centers of their eyes, crusting the dark centers. [This is good,] the meat worms say, blinking their soft eye folds. The crystals drop onto the undersides of their face. [Do you think we are beautiful now,] the organ meat worms ask. As their gemstones flutter, I admit they are beautiful. Maybe the crystals do work after all.

(My Vagina)

My bejeweled vagina prances across my face and it stinks of musk and raw crystals. [Join us in the sacred

vaginal place,] my vagina says as it pushes crystals out
of its crevice. [Crystals grow like fetal things,] it tells me.
[They latch onto the outside vaginal folds and filter feed
on the collected sweat.] [Is this normal,] I ask and the vagina folds together, then spreads apart like flower petals.
[That depends on your definition of vaginal normalcy,] it
says. My bejeweled vagina climbs into the nearest light
source and clings to the bulb. Its body trembles. The
jewels shine and sparkle. [I thought you were hungry,]
I say and the vagina crumbles around me. [Do you want
to wear me like a Mardi Gras mask?] my vagina asks. It
leaps off the bulb and clings to my face. I cannot get the
pulsing meat off. I scrape at the vagina with a wire hanger. I wipe its bulk with heavy sheets of steel wool. The
vagina does not come off my cheeks. I cut around my
jawbone and loosen my cheeks to get it off. [Does that
self surgery hurt,] my vagina asks, striking the floor in a
gallop. It gobbles the scissors out of my hands. Its white
crystals shine brilliantly. The glittering gems catch my
eyes and cut across my retinas with a laser beam of light.
[I need to cover you in dirt,] I say and throw flour at the
vagina. The vagina shrivels. The gemstones drop off. [A
yeast infection,] my vagina screams and it runs razors
along its outsides. It cuts all the hair pieces off. It leaves
raw skin ready for the crystals to grow against. [There
are starving children just outside the window,] I say,
throwing the crystals at the wall. My bejeweled vagina

glances at the glass panes. Skeletal children with sunken eyes stare through the frosted glass. They cup their small hands together. [Please, can we eat something,] the little children ask. The children drop to the floor begging. My vagina turns at my hips. It flares its lips and moistens its meat until the pink inner walls shine brilliantly. [No,] it says. [We like how shiny we look and we need all the food we can get to stay looking so trim.] My bejeweled vagina opens up again and removes several shrunken faces. The faces open their mouths and hold onto the vagina with their front teeth. [Get to work,] my vagina says as it twists slightly at the center. The faces stick their tongues out. They stretch and fold. They crunch the crystals. [Stop eating the rocks,] my bejeweled vagina screams. [And put those faces away.] The faces pop the skin with needles. They hold onto their tiny crystals with both hands. [This is not what I wanted,] my bejeweled vagina says. The dry faces hiss loudly. They salivate. The crystals drop off my vagina's skin as the adhesive loosens. [Stop this,] the crystal rocks scream. They move away from the bejeweled vagina in a single file. My bejeweled vagina follows behind them. [You were our most beautiful part of being bejeweled,] my vagina says. The crystals moan. They stick their inner tongues out. They flare the lips again and the stones turn around to stare. [We don't like how moist you are,] the crystals say. [You get us too wet.] The crystals slip through a crack beneath the door.

The vagina opens the door and stomp through behind them. [Come back,] my vagina says. [Crystals make me proud to be shaved bald.] When it catches up, it eats the crystals. Tiny mica flecks cling to the outsides of its lips as my vagina rotates from side to side, trying to decide on the best angle to see its sparkle. [We are so lovely,] my bejeweled vagina says. It pours wax down its center. It pulls a hair strip off. Crystal formations start to grow on the wounds again. [How pretty,] my vagina thinks.

(All of Me, Deux)

Anatomical cannibalism is prevalent throughout my body. It is in my bones and the longer my skin is left to its own devices, the more flesh it ingests even though my stomach is not made for self-consumption. [Stop doing this,] I say as I strike at my bowels with a hammer. There are pieces of a roasted sheep inside me. But my body does not want to eat it. There are also several heavy stones inside my stomach but my body refuses to split them in order to find the rotten egg hidden between them. I am sure that the rotten egg is making me sick. I bite at my wrists and the skin splits between my teeth, tearing down my arm and leaving a large gash occupied by a raw steak in my thighs. [Do I want to eat this?] I ask and my arms shove themselves into my mouth. I try to chew slowly but my mouth is not able to move, and so I just swallow instead. I lose weight even though I eat more and more of myself every day. I eat my body from the outside in and the skin does not get any warmer when moved around my mouth—it stays the same temperature. [There goes my stomach,] I say, pointing at the piece of meat that wavers between my teeth, then disappears, leaving a large gap just above my abdomen. I clap my hands and the organ meat looks skyward. [Do you remember the cannibalistic angels that used to visit us,] the organ meat asks. [They used to sit on our laps and steal the meat directly from our throats. And all we could do was grab our jaw and spread our mouths in two and allow them to feed from us. We had no choice. But upon reflection, it is obvious that it was all wrong. We hated how they tasted when they groped us. Make them go away, we used to say. Make them leave us alone, we pleaded. Do you remember that meat? It was so disgusting. Like vinegar. Like rotted faces. What will we do if we cannot get those terrifying faces out of us?] My organ meat stumbles over its words. I take several drugs meant for pain treatment and falling asleep. I make a drug cocktail. My organ meat walks down the street, trips, and face plants. [There, that's better,] my organ meat murmurs to itself, licking the sidewalk. [8, 9, 10. We are down for the count. Or we have no bones left to move around our mouths. Do we even have mouths? We have forgotten. What was the last thing that we ate?] My organ meat gently touches my neck. It licks the floor and attracts rocks with its mouth.

My wrists yearn to be cut as I watch it lying there. I stare into a mirror and see my colon appear from behind me. [There,] I say, pointing towards my colon. [That is my favorite body part. That is the best thing I own. Because it holds everything inside. It processes slowly and for me that is fine. It makes my body feel better, full. With everything I need inside me, I won't have to eat anymore. I will never be poisoned again.] Hearing me heap praise on my colon, my spleen disappears. It lodges itself in my throat. My throat clenches. [We must eat the flesh,] my skin says. [We are starving.] It wrinkles. It runs. It grabs my shoulders and shakes them. [You are a bad thing,] my skin says. [We will make you into a bucket of chum.] My organ meat pauses. It glances at the ceilings. It rests against the walls. [We do not actually know what chum is,] my organ meat says. [Are there aquatic beasts somewhere in the living room rug? Or are we making up the fins in our own heads?] My organ meat bares its teeth. It pushes itself into my body and sighs. [We are being digested,] my organ meat screams, lifting its flesh upward. It holds its flesh against my face. The organ meat crawls on the concrete, its heavy stone-flesh body dragging and coming apart with each step. [I think there used to be a piece of silver that kept us chained to the ground,] my organ meat says. My organ meat goes into the nearest basement. It throws itself into a meat chumer. It grinds itself up until thin fibers stack up, one on top of the other. [So tender,] the cannibal angels cry in delight. [When do we get more?]

(My Offal, Quatre)

My organ meat clings to my cremated companions. The dust swirls around its head until it creates a corpse halo. [This is wrong,] I say. The organ meat dips its wet roots into the powder bag and eats the dust up. [Delicious,] my organ meat whispers. [Now we can take another body into our own.] The organ meat eats the dust like fine confectionary sugar. The organ meat looks out onto a watery landscape and imagines the gray powder settling down on the waves, then disappearing. [Better that it live in my bowels,] I say. It rubs raw sand into its eyes. The organ meat dives into an ocean, moistening its flesh with salt water and grit. [All the better to eat one's self,] it says. It forces my mouth open and shoves dirt inside. My tongue twitches. I vomit and the organ meat crows like a murder of blackbirds. [We do not like this,] my organ meat says. My organ meat keeps a full urn beneath its pillow. [Who are you eating from?] I ask and the organ meat pauses with its head buried in the ceramic neck of the urn. The organ meat rises out slowly, its meats dusted over with pale powder. [It is just the toilet bowl,] the organ meat says. It pushes its head back into the urn and chews sullenly. [That is not the toilet bowl. Toilet bowls don't just fill with dust and dirt,] I say.

The organ meat comes out again. It spits the dust. [That's fine. Then this is a sink,] the organ meat says. [It is not a sink. Sinks don't just fill with dust.] I say. [Whatever meat it is, being dust like it is would mean that the meat was never solid to begin with. Or that it was tossed into an oven turned to such excruciatingly hot heat that it would just fall apart into pieces.] [That is that,] it says. [The oven was turned on and we pulled the sink from the fire without realizing that it was too late. That is that. This is simply our last saving grace,] my organ meat says. The organ meat rolls around the sink. It leaves a heavy grease slick on the outsides. [Somos cansados. Son polvos,] my organ meat says. It stumbles over the language. I knock the organ meat to the floor and cover the bloated torsos with sea salt grains. [Stop speaking to me like that,] I say. [I know what you are. I know what pieces of skin you've become.] My organ meat punches the walls. Its digestive parts burn with acid reflux. [We lost our hands,] the organ meat says. [You never had any sort of limb to begin with,] I say and the organ meat covers its face with its heavy flesh. It touches me. It strokes my arms. [Once upon a time, there was a girl who decided that she wanted meat but the flesh was too much for her bowels. And so, because she was so hungry but was not allowed to eat meat, she cut her own thighs and ingested them raw. Maybe, when she wanted to be more civilized, she held the meat over the fireplace until it cooked. Then she devoured it with some herbs and rosemary—no salt or pepper. But that was long ago. And now, she stands before us and asks that we eat from the processed things kept in her acid tubes,] the organ meats say. It dumps the urn's contents into its mouth. The organ meat chews slowly. [We have taken the entire body into our systems. We are the bodies. Through us the cadaver lives again,] the organ meat says. When it is finished, it tosses the urn to one side. I clap the organ meat on its back. [There,] I say. [Now you are full of powder.] The dust rises off its skin. I drag a knife across the stomach spilling the gray dust. Emptied, my organ meat sags like a rag doll.

Pickled Churches

Stained glass haloed church men absolve me for fucking my curling iron. [Thou shalt not have intimate, indecent relations with a creation of the domestic sphere,] the church men say spitting on the floor. They touch my hair, spindly fingers rubbing my glassine cheeks so hard that my skin ruptures. [You are free to urinate in our mouths. It is the only fluid we get but not everyone is so willing to spread their legs and take the piss out of us,] the church men say. They tilt back their hats and wait for me to climb onto their faces. I don't urinate on just any religious entity. I wear a veil over my face and tuck my rising bile into the back of my mouth while the church men's strings poke at my feet. [Won't you let us into the fertile lands in between your thighs,] the church men ask. [We have the rocking lap of a Bishop with your name on it.] In this, the realm where church men ask for urinary infections in their nasal passages, I run up and down wooden belfries and spread my knees for every bell-shaped dome that dares invade me. [We dong together. We ding as one. We tick and tock and chime.] I singsong. The church men stand on their hands. They break their heads against the railing shoulders and moan until their eyes bleed white wine. [It isn't even the sweet variety,] the church men shout. [It's so wrong. Bitterness twitching on the ends of our nervous tongues. Give us some of the glorious fecal matter at least. Our mouths are agape.] But my intestines are constipated. I need to use a rolling pin to get anything out. And I don't have any that aren't made of stainless steel, the only metal my digestive system has trouble processing in its kidney stone pits. [Thou shalt not deny us the skin we've dreamed of wearing,] the church men say. [If we want a mask, you have to give it to us.] The priests scratch my chin. The priests bite my forehead. [Give it to us,] they shout. [We want a few bites. Or we want to lose our muscles. We need to eat something that is feminine.] I climb the bell. I hide inside the bulb. I bang against the sides until my ears go deaf. [I don't care about sound,] I say. [It only matters that I keep my hands to my eyes.] I pluck my eyelids. I scorch my brows. The church men play with bronchial strands hanging down from the calcified chandeliers. [Take this with your defecation,] the church men say and toss the elastic threads at my face. The bells bat the flesh away. The bells strike the church men in their chins.

Church men, with their stained cheeks and teeth, drop over the railing and fall five hundred feet into the sub-basement where little trolls hang their legs and weep for the sacramental monsters sleeping between their toes. [Church men,] they ask. [For us to eat? How delectable.] They sink their canines into the shins and scratch skin off bone. Legs go numb as the troll things chew. The church men stick blue planks into the backs of their mouths and block their throat entrances. [We don't need a single meaty thing,] the church men say. [We have our glass shards and our protein bowels, the constant crystallized roots spreading in our jaws. Who wants a mandibular reaction when there are so many little naked girls and boys in the world?] I go to my curling iron and plug it in. I caress its warming flanks and when I insert it between my breasts, my bloody burns turn yellow. The ruined flesh knocks the church men palms down. [Sanctify,] the stained church men screams.

The Uterus Dies

The uterus cries over dead elephants. [The poor tusks,] the uterus says. The uterus looks under the beds for a little trunk but only finds mounds of dust bath material. [Why did the elephants dream of grassy plains when they were stuffed inside rotten lion manes,] the uterus asks snorting and spraying mucus over a painted bedroom mirror. [And this is why the fleece suffers from a urinary infection,] the uterus says as it milks itself into a wine glass. The uterus holds the fluid up to the light and licks the glass stem. [I am not impressed by the coloration, it looks infected] the uterus says. It climbs out of a window and lands in a drainage ditch. Solid filth clings to the endometrium. Fecal water drains from blistered red tubes. [There was a twisted colon once. But I am more concerned with the convoluted cervix. That is the more lethal affliction. And the longer the hungry egg cells sit on the wall, the more liable they are to break down and

fall,] the uterus says. It parts the coarse hair swathing its vulva and removes a trash bag from tucked behind its spinal base. [Do we know each other,] the uterus asks. It pushes a rusted fork into its womb partition and rolls its tongue along the floor. [Dusty,] the uterus says. It walks several feet before collapsing into a pool of radioactive fluid. It pokes its heaving sides. [What will happen to me when my family comes to dispose of my corpse? I am a contamination sack. As soon as I touch the floor, uranium ions drop from my flesh and roll into attic corners,] the uterus says. It lies flat in the puddle until its flesh wrinkles. [Ah, wonderful. The eggs are fertilized. Now I can give birth without any thought to the mammary repercussions,] the uterus says. It pushes out five hard-boiled eggs and breaks the shells off each one. [Compliments to the slightly poached yolk,] the uterus says and cuts the eggs into quarters. The uterus turns in a circle. It stubs a stump on a rusted pipe. The uterus pitches forward. Rotted blades cut the uterus into several thick chunks. Gloved hands roll the pieces in plastic wrap and place them in a refrigerated container. [Will you sell us like steak,] the pieces ask. The hands stamp prices over the uterine chunks. [Blue,] the uterine chunks scream. [We hate blue! Where is the red? What about the purple, the pink? Anything but blue. Or green. Both are so unhealthy.] The pieces gray. Bile seeps out. It collects around the plastic wrap edges. [We are not meant to be fried,] the uterine chunks say. [We get gummy when floured and placed into boiling oil. And do not even think of treating us like onion sautéed steaks. We don't take on those flavors. We have our own. We don't like root vegetables to begin with.] The chunks eat the packaging and slip onto the floor. They stare up at the ceiling and glance down dirty aisles. [There used to be elephants here,] the uterine chunks say. [They were young elephants barely able to breathe on their own so predators adopted them and carried the fat little elephants on their backs.] The uterine chunks sob. They flood hallways and closets. [Poor elephants,] they moan.

The uterus will die in a desert, after the uterus has traveled for years searching for some form of lactation it can never find. [Milk,] the uterus will whisper as it is dying rubbing its strange udder protrusions against the sand dunes, nudging them to produce any form of fluid the uterus can drink. This is all because the uterus will forget how dry sand is, how far away the ocean is. Even now, long before its death, it still goes to the wrong places, dragging its womb parts, moaning into sewer grates and picking at fence chains, trying to find a gallon or a quart. [I just want a bit to sip,] the uterus says and runs broken glass shards across its tubes. [Yes, this is the process of tubal ligation and I am far from ashamed that I am constantly made infertile by my own walls. I do not wish to achieve any sort of swelling. The monthly bleeding is bad enough.] When the uterus dies, it will be because the uterus has forgotten how to shed its skin and will attempt to rub itself on rusted plates in order to scrape off the thick lining. [I am not the womb you think I am,] it will say and pitch itself off a building roof to land splattered on a far below sidewalk. When the uterus dies, there will be blood stains everywhere, deep pools extending half a mile because the uterus is less of a uterus and more of a blood bag. [Use me in your transfusions,] the uterus will say to infected prostitutes, before it runs away. It cannot stand IV stands or dull needles. [Do not even attempt to press into my only arteries. These passageways are mine alone to fill with sandwiches, only then will I eat away,] the uterus says. It stomps its stump and sits in a yellowed open-all-the-time diner, its ends barely touching the moist ground. [Coffee,] the uterus says at the sagging mouth of the waitress, [No milk.] The uterus never drinks its coffee dark and without sugar. It knocks the table over and slides out the door, streaking the floor with deep amber seepage. [Ho ho ho, I'm the bovine thingy,] the uterus sings. As it comes closer to the death door it can smell the abattoir rot. When the uterus dies, it will be because a man could not separate the uterus from steak and instead he threw both into a pan for his late-night meal. [I am hungry,] the man will say and dust the bovine uterus with granulated garlic until the meat reeks. And so the uterus will hang limply in the heat. It will heap itself onto a plate and seize up when the man begins cutting. [I only wanted a drink of milk,] the uterus will say. But the uterus will not die because the plate is not a desert. The desert is also not the lining that the uterus will have trouble removing from its bulk. But this is all ahead of the uterus. Now, it just sits on the dirty ground, trying to remember when it first noticed anyone whistling its name, then making several crude gestures with a paper bag. The uterus cries over the obscenities. It makes its own milk but the fluid is tasteless and smells like water. [I am leaking,] the uterus moans. It lies on its side and looks away from the gathering crowd. [I am not meat,] the uterus shouts. But everyone who looks immediately thinks, [Cow.]

Sometimes, the uterus imagines a world where the uterus has received a hysterectomy and is no longer the womb-creature wandering the streets, leaking old poisons and a variety of dead things. [Do not be surprised,] the uterus says. [I have diarrhea but that is nothing. Look at all the septic fluids seeping out of my pinholes.] The uterus points to the tiny prick marks covering its tissues. [They are akin to pores,] the uterus says. It bleats and wipes its frontal walls. [That was an accident,] the uterus says. [I did not mean to make such a mess out of myself. Look. The mucus drips out of me so quickly; I become dehydrated within a matter of seconds. My own blood cells cannot reproduce fast enough to make up for this seepage. But I move on. Give me milk and I will come back to life.] Its backside withers. The flesh puckers with dry wrinkles and the uterus says, [The men cut me into chunks, then stitched all the tube parts closed but I can still defecate without any problems. Look, the fecal matter streams out of my upper parts and it drops just fine. This is because I am infected with a belly infection that does not make sense to anyone but me. Because I am a womb. Perhaps instead of forced menopause, I simply ate tainted meat without remembering and contracted mad cow disease. Maybe this is why they call me COW. These things have happened before, I am sure of it. I cannot keep myself contained in a latex bag for the duration of my lifetime. Yes, my various orifices hurt as I give up the solid waste within my bowels but that is nothing. I have been cut up and made to produce before.] The womb peels dirty bandages off its bottom. It tosses the adhesive strips into a torn pillowcase and wipes the fabric against the back of its vase-like neck. [I am used to feeling the ovulation twitches. But there is something nice about the stability in my walls. It is as if I have abandoned a fault line for solid ground and no longer have to worry about my foundation shaking so hard that it collapses. I feel renewed. This menopause is not as problematic as I initially imagined it might be,] the uterus says. It sneezes and a blood slick drops out of the womb and onto the tiled floor. [This does not feel good,] the uterus says. [I had

expected some sort of numbing sensation but this moisture is a bit too much.] The uterus sags and drags licking a puddle of thumbtacks. [My tongue blisters when I
touch the sharp points,] the uterus says. It pulls a piece
of fabric out of its neck and wraps it around the stemmed
stump. [I am resilient enough to know that I can always
reverse these fertility procedures. It is just a matter of
matching the bloody fibers up,] the uterus says. It grows
a hoof in the center of its digestive bulk and pokes at the
enamel protrusion. [I am a true bovine now,] the uterus says. It milks the hoof into a crystal tumbler. Amber
marrow pours out of the hoof. It fills the glass half-way.
The uterus leans over the glass. It breathes deeply and
sips. [It is clear that I might have sustained life with this
but I'd rather be the one who drinks it,] the uterus says.

The uterus walks along abandoned city streets, dragging its stumps and searching for any sort of glass piece
it might rake across its bulk in an act of severance. It faces a factory with broken windows and a shadowed man
standing in each frame. [Come to your knees,] the men
wail and reach for the uterus. The uterus sits on the curb
and watches the men curiously. [Are you actually made
of flesh,] the uterus asks. The men's heads melt into the
window frames. [We believe we are. We are... material,]
the men say hesitantly. Their skin fuses with the wood so
that they become windows with limbs. [Do you see,] the
men ask. [This is how we really are. We are so wonder-

ful, being made from organic materials. No one can hurt us. Just use a saw to cut us if you are angry. Or torch us with a gallon of gasoline.] The men scratch their armpits. Flaky skin floats to the ground. The uterus lifts the flesh up and presses it against its tissue. [Look,] the uterus says. [New material to shed. This is wonderful. Now I can go through my menstrual cycle without losing my skin. All that matters is that I shed any bit of unnecessary flesh. And so I will give this meat away first.] The uterus plucks the dead flesh from its frontal portions. Red blisters coat the outer skin. [Come visit the factories,] the men say. Their voices come out of the rusted nails. They wave their hands and feet. Their bodies lift into the air, then drop back down, humming while their necks bend and snap. [I do not want to have anything to do with that sort of industry,] the uterus says. [I cannot stand the heat associated with factories. And I am not so naive that I do not realize that these buildings are all broken down. There are no real factories to speak of. Look, I can see that the smoke stacks stopped billowing a long time ago. The pipes are coated with ashy residue. There is no production. You simply want me to go into that industrialized body so that you might tear me into pieces you can toss around.] It stands up. The men pull their heads out of the wood frames. The wood cracks. The buildings turn dark gray. Their edges melt. Tar and liquid brick drip onto the sidewalks. The uterus stares at the puddles of raw materials. [I have no desire to be eaten. Or to be sown with your seeds so that you can have your progeny come to term. This womb is closed. Just as that factory is closed. Just like your heads are closed. You have needles protruding from your eyes and that is not right. Nor is the way your pus bits well up in the corners of your eyes and leave yellowed streaks along your faces,] the uterus says. It drags its bulk down the street. The men jump from the windows and place their faces in the slick. They walk with their heads down and their backs arched, snorting the fluids up their nostrils. Their lungs swell. At the street corner, the uterus pauses. It removes the steak chops from its sides and throws them at the men. The shadowy figures grab the meat up and hold it to their mouths. They pitch to one side. [A dry drowning,] they say and die.

Many people are surprised when the uterus decides to refrain from breeding. [Why don't you want your body to achieve its full potential,] they ask. The uterus pokes its flesh bits and removes several layers of old walls. [Well, I do not think I should be forced to shrink and grow. I prefer my body as it is. The flesh wants to stay in one place and I do not think the pain is worth the parasite clinging to my innards,] the uterus says. [After all, would you go through so much trouble to house a tapeworm?] The uterus slips away. The people pat its sides. [But there are so many things that come out of reproducing,] they say [Babies, for one.] The uterus climbs a wall. It bleeds. The blood pours out and floods several households. [Do not treat me like a factory. I detest factories. They are filthy and hot and too many people have blistered hands beneath their thin gloves. And the broken windows. And the smoke stacks. I hate them all. I will never produce anything connected to factories. Neither a pipe nor a wrench. Not even a child. I refuse. They are all smelly, greasy things and my womb will remain hermetically sealed even without receiving any semblance of ko-sher approval. I give my approval and that is enough,] the uterus says. The uterus hits the floor several times, breaking tiles up and tossing asbestos powder into the air. [Do not go. Do not make sense. Do not breed. Do not, do not, do not. For I do not want to be made into anything less than what I am,] the uterus says. [I know that there are many of my kind who constantly stretch and shrink. But not I. I refuse because I want something more exciting. I want to keep my stitches in place and not have latex gloves force more needles into me.] The people pour lemon juice over the womb. They stroke the sides and use razor blades to pick the thick walls clean. [All you have to do is lie back and relax,] the people say. [After all, conception will happen when you least expect it. And all you need to know is that stitches are a part of life. You take the needles in and that is the end of it. You will grow back to how you were. Then you can give birth again and continue the cycle. You are an elastic band. You stretch, then return to your original shape. Because that is how good you are. That is what your legacy is.] The uterus growls. It grows horns. It rams people through their chests, then tosses them to one side so that it can pass. [I do not want to breed,] the uterus says. [I am my own womb. I want to stay empty. I just want to exist. You cannot make me do anything I lack the strength to do.] It snarls several times and everyone backs away. The uterus whacks its backside against a metal pore and develops a silver patina over its sides. [I am metal now,] the uterus lies. [Look at how the elemental things grow upon me. I cannot breed. I am probably radioactive. What a shame. I am moving on.] The uterus slides to one side. The people grab at its vase neck. The uterus plugs its holes with oranges. [There is no room,] it says.

To keep the hyenas away, the uterus soaks in a tub of vinegar, pickling the uterine walls to the very point of softness. [I can't trust these beasts. They live off meat and so I must make mine nearly inedible,] the uterus says. It lifts its bulk out of the vinegar bath and slides through an abandoned parking structure. [I am below ground,] the uterus whispers. It trips over a rock and falls into a car. Hyenas come around the corner. They wear concrete penises on their heads. [Hee, hee, hee,] the hyenas laugh rubbing their coarse fur against the uterus. To keep safe from the beasts, the uterus has large spines sticking out of its flesh. [Try to eat me,] the uterus says and knocks into the hyenas. They bleed out on the floor, their faces pale and twisted beneath the thick fur. The uterus scratches its back. It stumbles up several ramps. A trail of pale fluid marks its movements. [I wish I were dry but that would just lead to other complications, the uterus says. The parking lot reeks of vaginal fluid. [I was not here before,] the uterus says. It ducks behind rusted vehicles and licks the flat tires until old tissue slips out of the walls. The uterus knocks the tissue to the side and moves on. Red clots fill the parking garage. They rise out of the ground. The hyenas step in them and turn around in quick circles, trying to snap at their own legs to get the meat off. [We are hungry,] the hyenas howl. They paw at the ground and the uterus scales a foundation pillar. It climbs to the top and clings to the ceiling. The hyenas move around below, scratching at their flea-filled ears and pausing from time to time to yank rotted flesh out of the rubble. Bones clatter down a ramp and the hyenas run after the dried calcium logs, leaving the uterus alone. Safe, the uterus drops down again. It keeps its back against concrete sides, scraping its flesh on the walls. [I ovulate daily. This is fine,] the uterus whispers under its breath. It glances around one corner, looking for the hyenas. The beasts paw the ground and look in the sneaking uterus's direction. They snap their jaws. They stick their paws into their mouths and chew violently. The uterus

stands still. [You won't eat me,] the uterus whispers. It
drops through a hole in the floor, landing in a sewerage
system. The hyenas circle the hole but do not jump after
it. They do not like water. The uterus sits below ground,
nursing its wounds and menstruating three separate
times in one week. Blood fills the sewers. The uterus
hangs thin tissue curtains up on the walls, decorating the
mildewed stone. [It is like home,] the uterus whispers. It
listens to the scratching above it, as the hyenas push cars
over to get at the meat underneath. They bite the stone,
breaking their teeth but still thinking there is flesh in the
pillar centers. What they smell is just the uterus's fertility stench. It is like steak. The uterus soaks itself in the
waste water. [I wonder what scum parasites are here,]
the uterus says. It collects tainted rainwater with its lips.

The uterus is experimental. [[[[[[[[[[[[fertility]]]]]]]]]]]]]
[It sits amongst us,] says the uterus, grabbing at its sick
ends. [There once was a chicken that ate an egg. it was a
cannibal. It committed a pinnacle fertility sin,] the chick-
en moans. The uterus moans and throws its walls around,
splattering the bed sheets with blood. [I knew other lan-
guages, a long time ago when I was just a cell cluster,]
the uterus says. [But look at me now. I am just walls and
tissue pieces and conception clumps. Who wants me?]
the uterus asks. [Men don their gloves and oil my joints
and weld my fuses and act as if I am a factory. Breeding
chain. I am a woman. I am a womb, the uterus says.] [I

am a woman but I am not just a woman,] the uterus says. <<<I am a uterus.>>> <<<I am a womb uterus.>>> <<<I am the bovine uterus.>>> [Watch me and I will make you think of steak,] the uterus rains. The uterus pours. It fills buckets with moisture. Trashcans float away in a stream of the uterus's favorite fluids. [You cannot tame me,] the uterus says. <<<I am bovine. Hear me moo.>>> Famous men paint pictures of the uterus's flesh and each one comes out bloody and smeared. [That is you just behind that wall,] the men say, pointing at parts of the uterus illustration. But the uterus is not pleased. [I am not pleased,] the uterus says. [Why do you think I am so smeared? I am a compact creature. I am not dripping and made of hazy curves. Why do you think that? Is it because you are hungry for flesh and I am the closest protein source you can get to?] The uterus bites. <<<Hail the uterus>>> The uterus surrounds many artistic men and gives them a claustrophobic feeling in their chests. [I am not meat,] the uterus says. It hisses. It strings men up by their feet and suspends them over a mucus bath. [Do not act like I am beneath you. I do not need to be painted to be remembered. Everyone in this world knows some form of uterus. Mine is just the most visible,] the uterus says. The uterus chews. It chews the air. It chews the dirt. A man puts a finger between the uterus's lips and suffers a split joint. [I will eat you, too,] the uterus says. The men paint the uterus again. [This is too dark,] the bovine uterus screams.] The men are scared. They give the uterus yellow undertones. But yellow always makes the uterus look sickly. [You cannot hurt me that way,] the uterus says. It picks up a brush and paints the men with its fermenting tissue. [The uterine wine,] the uterus says and it gives the men large mouths with foaming tongues. It paints quickly, transforming the men from stick figures into irate bloodbaths. [I am disgusted,] the bovine uterus says. [Just disgusted.] It tears the canvas into two parts. It throws the men out on the streets. They crawl home. The bovine uterus sits on its favorite plush paper chair and scratches its outsides. [I am not so smeared,] the bovine says.

A chicken pecks the expanse of the uterus's front lawn until the ground is pockmarked with many holes and the chicken screams through the dirt mouthfuls. [Why did the uterus shed its lining,] the uterus asks. It waits for the chicken to open its beak before telling the punch line. [Because it was tired of the weight,] the uterus says. It is not a comedian. It is a uterus trying to poke fun at its own body. The chicken picks at its feathers, then it resumes pecking at the dirt. [Why was the chicken so afraid of the dirt,] the uterus asks. [Because it didn't want a deep fried dirt coating.] It chuckles and the chicken stares. [For your information, the chicken jokes barely work with a punch line. Think of something more original,] the chicken says, nibbling an ear of corn. The uterus kicks the chicken in its breast. [There once was a chicken that was really a man made out of straw and feathers. But he was a poultry fiend and so when he got the first whiff of his new body odor, he salivated. Then the man invited himself into a frying pan. He ate his toes first, then the little chicken wings attached to his armpits. He chewed through the searing pain and barely blinked when his blood mixed with the oiled pan drippings. The man kept whispering about what delicious fried chicken he had at his disposal. Everyone was jealous. They asked him to share. He was greedy and ate himself all up,] the uterus says. The chicken shrugs. [I've heard worse things. Plus, that isn't the only chicken byproduct to eat itself. We all have a few bites before other people come to fry us up in thick pieces,] the chicken says. It pecks the ground again, tossing stones and worms into the air. The uterus wiggles back and forth, trying to catch the debris in its vase top. [Then you tell your joke,] the uterus says. The chicken swallows a mouthful of grain. [What do you call a womb that barely remembers to bleed,] the chicken asks. [What,] the uterus asks. [A menoterus,] the chicken says. It pauses and pulls a few feathers out from beneath its beak. [Get it? Because it is a uterus that is menopausal? No? I tried. I'm a chicken. All I'm supposed to do is eat. Why are you making me tell these jokes,] the chicken says. It pecks at the ground again and lays an egg on an anthill. [And now my shells will become infected by protozoans,] the chicken moans. It stomps the egg into the ground, shattering the shell. Bright yellow yolk runs along the ground. Ants run after it. They gather the protein strands in their mouths and carry the droplets home. The chicken looks up. [You want a joke? Here's one. A chicken ran off the dinner table and hopped into a cab. And the men inside, all drunk and hungry, took one look at the bird and tore its breast from its legs. Then they ate the chicken up and braided the feathers into their nappy hair,] the chicken says. [That is the moral of the story. Everyone will come to eat me eventually. Because I am destined for the dinner plate. And you are meant to go dry.] It pecks again. The uterus dilates. It swallows the chicken up.

A ghostly thing touches the uterus's top and base and chills the blood-lined tissue to the point of shedding. [Are you a man or a woman,] the uterus asks and the ghost thing just nods its head up and down. It drops its hands to its genital joints and although there is smoothness, there is no slit. It is not a female. And without the small erection appendage, it is not a male. The uterus scratches the ghost and draws its own blood. [You've made me bleed,] the uterus says and the ghost thing shrugs. [I have no blood to give away,] the ghost thing says. The uterus rubs itself against greasy walls. It leaves dark burgundy smears against the plaster. [This wallpaper should be reformed,] the uterus says. [It is a sick thing. The paper just slips off. It pools on the floor. It is not right.] The uterus pushes the paper back onto the walls. [Don't you have any glue within you,] the uterus asks. The ghostly thing presses against the wallpaper but its misty body slips through the material. [I don't have enough substance to my body to give the paper the adhesive qualities you desire it to have,] the ghostly thing says. The uterus sighs. It slaps the ghostly thing around and the mist develops a faint red tinge. [Stop injuring me. It feels so terrible. I do not want to be anything less than a solid entity,] the ghostly thing says. The ghostly thing prances down a hallway, dragging its spinal bones behind. The uterus follows after, clinging to the jutting thigh bones. [Do you know how often I shed,] the uterus asks. [The walls just come down. Sometimes, I am barely a part of my own body. I am distanced from it. I enjoy the flowing red though it makes me sick. I become anemic whenever my body comes apart.] The uterus releases the ghostly thing and lies back on the floor. It stares at the ceiling. It picks at its outer flesh. [Whenever nails rake against me, I bleed outwardly. But all the important liquid proteins stay inside my tissue bits,] the uterus says. It cracks its top against the floor until the boards splinter. The ghostly thing turns around. It walks over the uterus. The uterus feels cold. It grabs at its bulging center and smoothes the skin until it numbs. [Do not resist the fact that I am pure energy. I come out of the outlets. When you bleed, I am that cystic electricity. I spark red and blue,] the ghostly thing says. It kicks at the flesh piled up beneath the table. The uterus watches the abuse. [I think that is a piece of skin I misplaced some time ago,] the uterus says. [But that happens. I let it go and it slipped away and found itself a dark crevice to exist within. Sometimes, it needs to remain in the shadows. It develops a burn no amount of aloe can cure. Something like muscle cancer. Or a fleshy obtrusion.] The ghostly thing settles on the ground beside the uterus. It pets the uterine flesh and whimpers softly. [I thought that I might push myself in a cavernous body but even those spaces are cramped,] the ghostly thing says and lactates.

A harmonious war pushes through the uterus's inner chambers and gives the womb indigestion. [I am a pacifist and this is not the kind of peace arrangement I had expected,] the uterus says. The uterus rubs its stitched up tubes and yanks hard-boiled eggs out of the pipes. [This is some sort of melodic tragedy,] the uterus says. It pulls its tubes out of its head and drops them onto the ground. [There. Tubal ligation. I do not need these little faucets. After all, I want my walls to shed for an entire lifetime and see no need in letting the tissue parts thicken. And so here, my hysterectomy, so that no man can ever say I am dramatic just because of anatomical correspondences,] the uterus says. It throws the worm-like tubes into a trash can. Before replacing the lid, the uterus stares at the curling pipes. [It is a shame that these were not made of copper. Otherwise, I might have recycled them and made some good money,] the uterus says. It pushes the lid over the garbage can and slides away. Today, of all days, the fluid is pale orange instead of red. The uterus retraces its steps, sliding back over its previous trails, changing the fluid from pale tangerine to a brighter tangor. [Oh dear god,] the uterus says, clutching its frontal parts. [What is happening? I can't understand why orange is falling out. And it smells. Like rotten meat. Oh, oh, oh god.] It kicks at the trails, smearing them. The uterus turns and goes to the nearest store. It pulls lemons out of the produce bins and cuts them into wedges. The uterus plugs its sides up with the sour fruits and breathes deeply. It stares down at its trails and watches the orange pool up around it. [What does all this orange mean to me,] the uterus says. [This is some brutal fertility. Or productive infertility. Or something. I don't even know anymore. I am so confused and the lemon oil seeps into my head and makes me think of tropical forests. Am I a uterus that used to belong to a mangrove tree?] The uterus pitches to one side. It shudders. It strikes its top against the ground. [I'd prefer there to be some form of red. Or pink. Or even brown. A more natural fluid. Nothing is orange within me,] the uterus shrieks. It turns around and twists at its base. The uterus throws the lemons out and replaces their space with red

fruits. The uterus sucks in strawberries cherries rasp-
berries and grapes. It plugs its walls up. The red skins
push out of the tissue. Juice drips down the inner walls.
[Red,] the uterus cries and climbs onto a pile of red
grapefruits. Vermillion fluid seeps out of the uterus and
wets the fruits. They turn redder and the uterus laughs.
[I have reduced the orange,] it says. [I made the other
colors go away.] It lifts its head again and stares at the
small shadowed figure standing by its bottom. [What do
you want,] the uterus asks. The figure points at the fruit.
The uterus throws the vegetation. [Take your blossoms,
all these hard-skinned wombs. I don't need them,] the
uterus says. Orange eggs drop in the bin.

The uterus smells of spring rain. [Do you smell the
freshness,] it asks the radiators. The uterus plucks at its
sagging sides and pushes them into the metal structures.
The radiators try to sniff but only manage to steam. [It
must be some sort of condensation,] the radiator says.
[Maybe it is something akin to pond scum.] The uterus
kicks the frontal part and stubs its tubes. [That is just
cruel. Pond scum. You couldn't even equate me with a
flowing body of water. You know that my identity relies
on the ability to shed things. If I am a menstrual thing,
then I am a coursing fluid thing,] the uterus says. The radiator overflows. Water fills the room. The uterus floats
on its back and rubs against the ceiling. [This room is
so... pedestrian,] the uterus grumbles. The radiator

slurps its fluids back up. The metal shines brightly. The uterus drops to the floor and reaches to touch the heated aluminum sides. [I am not impressed by your fertility,] it says. It kicks the radiator and stubs its tissue base. [I have injured myself and now cannot breathe correctly,] the uterus says. The womb climbs into the radiator and sits on top of the heating joints. [These wires,] the uterus says, plucking at the cables snaking around the radiator's innards. [Are they some form of artery? Is there a heart in there? Or some kind of metal uterus like my own?] The radiator lifts off the floor. It spider crawls away from the uterus. The uterus runs after it. The uterus leaps onto the radiator and clings to the metal. It rolls around and pitches back and forth. [This is an unruly ride,] the uterus says. Water seeps out of the uterus and fills the radiator. [This is far from enjoyable,] the uterus says. [This is even less enjoyable than that,] the radiator responds. It snaps its cables and water pours out of the metal. [Are you giving birth,] the uterus asks, still rocking with the radiator's movements. [Yes,] the radiator shouts. [I am birthing a tea kettle. I will name it Maximus and it will be the best creature in the world. Now, look. It is storming outside and I should be turned off but I am not.] The radiator groans and dribbles. [I instinctively know what the labor is like,] the uterus says. [Now just breathe and your metal flesh will spread apart and let the new body through. And do not stop breathing because as soon as you stop your lungs, the body will get stuck, then you will hurt.] The uterus sprays the radiator with oil and other lubricants. It spreads melted butter on the sides. It vomits mucus over the rusted base. [Just breathe,] the uterus says. It sniffs the air frantically. [Do you smell that thick meat odor,] the uterus asks. It tears the radiator sides open. The radiator steams. It wets the uterus's sides. The uterus pulls the wires out. It reaches around the metal cogs and files its digits against the roughest metal parts. [I can't stop thinking about the smell,] the uterus says. It solders the radiator and melts the metal. The uterus moves through the rubble. It sniffs. [Oh, the steak was just me,] it says.

The uterus pretends to be an angler fish. Fertile men rub against the uterine sides and smell the odor of a sizzling steak. They bite the uterus and their mouths melt off. Goodbye, mouth parts. Goodbye, little lip joints. The men fuse to their angler mother and become her reproductive sacs. [Because I only need you to fertilize me,] the uterus says. [That way I don't have to feed you. You aren't worthy of sharing any of my meals. So move away. Become a thorn in my side and a pin in my fin and that is it. Testicle beast. Cell monster.] The uterus cuts tiny gills into its sides and throws itself into a glass of water. It drifts to the bottom of the glass and hovers just above the glass pane. [I keep men stored within me,] the uterus laughs. It pokes at the men living inside its sides. The men try to bite but their teeth fall out. They lose their tongues to the thick uterine walls. The men whimper. Then they lose their voices. The walls suck the noise up and thicken. [It is like blood,] the uterus says. But the bovine uterus barely knows what it is really saying. It touches the men lumps and stabs each protrusion with a pair of tweezers. [I thought this might be a cyst. But apparently, I'm wrong. Because this has no interior. There is no bile filling. So sad. I wanted to pop it open and collect the fluid on a dirty diner napkin,] the uterus says. It scratches the cysts, dislodging one and tossing it onto the floor. Slowly, the uterus extends a tube and grinds the cyst into the ground, leaving a stain on the linoleum tiles. [Fly away to the other ends of the world, where the uterus grows and the little men melt into balls filled with sperm,] the uterus sings. It flicks its backside around in the air. The uterus pulls at the men lumps. [Did you enjoy eating away at my flesh,] it asks. The lumps grumble. The uterus rubs against an open bottle of acetone, spilling it onto the men chunks. The boils shriek. They scoot around, trying to gain distance between themselves and the body but because they are attached, they form a red rash. [Aren't you sorry for those selfish acts,] the uterus asks. The chunks mumble. The uterus scratches them again. [I'll get you all freeze-dried off,] the uterus says. It vomits up a mouthful of the sperm seeping out of the lumps and into the uterus's bowels. [I am less than impressed by your fertility,] the uterus says. [Someone said that to me once and I didn't realize what it meant. But now I do. Because fertility tastes bad. I do not want to lose the sensation of cold in my tissue walls.] The uterus pulls a cheese grater out of a drawer. It rubs the rasp over the boils, scraping them off. The men fall to the floor. They try to attach to the dirt but there aren't any parasitic teeth for them to hold on with. The men fall over. They wriggle but their limbs are gone. The uterus rubs its tubes against its openings, removing the men's flesh. [Don't wither,] the uterus says but the men do.

Men shackle the uterus's tubes together and leave the tissue on a metal examining table. [You're meat,] the men say. The uterus slides out of the chains and throws the metal onto the floor. [I am a uterus. Not beef,] the uterus says. It moos and slaps its tubes against the ground, breaking the tiles and throwing chipped parts into the air. The pieces strike the men in the eyes. [Oh, we've lost our vision,] the men cry. They pull metal shards out of the mucus membranes. The whites split and ooze. The uterus slides over the moisture and sucks the fluids up. [You taste like pure sucrose,] the uterus says. It kicks the men in the ankles. The men fall into the chains. Their bones shatter and break. The uterus pushes its tubes into the wounds and prods the calcium until it moves out of place. [Now there is no need for marrow,] the uterus says. [You are just empty bone parts and the fat is meant to be pushed into tin buckets and dipped in wax. That is just lovely. I will put those pieces in between bread slices and eat them up like a sandwich.] The men fall to their knees. The uterus opens its womb. The flesh cuts and pieces back together. [We could break your womb into parts,] the men shout. The uterus screams and strikes its head with a metal hammer. [Don't treat me like a concrete pillar. I am a living thing,] the uterus says. It jumps on top of the men's chests and breaks the ribs. They crush the bones and enamel powder comes out of their nostrils. It dusts over their lips and drops into their mouths. The men choke. They cough. They stick their tongues out and the muscles go dry. [We hurt,] the men say. The uterus takes a pair of garden shears to the tongues and clips the ends off. [Now you don't have any facial appendages to molest women with,] the uterus says. It giggles and pours battery acid over the stomachs. The chests cave in. The skin collapses. The uterus digs its tubes in and pulls the flesh apart. [I can make you all into uteruses, too,] the uterus says. It stitches the bone fragments up. It braids the nerve endings. It plucks the ligaments out of the appendages and throws them into a trash can. It jumps into the bag and compresses the meat into a box. [There. Now you can have ovaries and hatch your unfertilized eggs,] the uterus says. It spits on the ground. It rubs muscle juice over the metal slabs. The room reeks of copper water. The men lift their heads. [We do not want to be females,] the men say. [We are unprepared to give birth in any manner. And sometimes, we have labor nightmares and small dolls drop out of us but we do not know what to do with them.] The uterus slaps the men across their fat cheeks and leaves red welts all over their flesh. [I think that your eyes will drop out of your sockets one day,] the uterus says. It sneezes over the men. The men scratch their armpits and elbows. [We're burning,] the men say. The uterus slips out of the room. It dreams of metal pipes and tables. It wishes for fabric bed parts.

The uterus loses its walls and walks around, an empty womb of a thing. It shoves hangers down its neck and feels around, trying to nudge the sharp end against some tissue wall but the sides have been scraped clean. [I've been butchered,] the uterus moans. It slaps its fat against plaster boards until the drywall cracks. [Oh, my poor menstruation. What do I do with myself now? I can't bleed and so that means I am menopausal but I am too young to have unusable parts,] the uterus says. It growls and groans. The uterus sits on a porch and pretends it is a beast going to slaughter. It dodges dropping blades and shudders until its outer flesh layers fall off its body. The uterus kicks the skin away. [It is a costume,] the uterus says. [It is an interesting piece of flesh I can play with. I can sew it into a leather sack and place it on my vase head. It is fun. Like a toy.] The uterus steps on the bag until the sides tear. It wanders into a slaughterhouse and

rubs against the razor walls. [I am open,] the uterus cries.
[I am wide open and no one can sew me shut. Oh, this
is not the ideal existence but I am pleased regardless.]
The uterus jumps into an electrified pool and swims laps
while its flesh charges. Its womb glows with radioactive
blue light. [Pump me full of vitamins,] the uterus shouts.
Gel capsules fall from the ceilings and into the uterus's
opening. The uterus fills up. It crushes the capsules and
sucks the dust up. [Oh, my head is swelling, spinning,
swirling. I don't know what galaxy I am a part of. Look,
there are ovarian stars and I wish my tubes would fill
with dusty bits,] the uterus says. It vomits onto the old
razor blades and the metal rusts up. The room spins and
the uterus slaps the dimensions into separate planes. The
uterus hops from blade to blade, then pushes through
a peeling machine. Cogs strip the thin placenta off the
uterus's sides. The uterus pops out nude on the opposite end. [Happiness, finally,] the uterus says. [This is too
much like Zen. Or something akin to a grill. I can cook
up my own ovaries and leave them for the manglers to
dine on.] The uterus screeches. It darts past the meat
hooks and swings from the pointed ends. Its sides stick
to the curves and yank off. [I am so injured and the blood
trails move around the room for the butchers to follow
but that is not a problem. After all, these areas reek of
protein but how will any of the hunters know it is me,]
the uterus says. It darts into a frozen closet and its flesh

turns purple with frostbite. The tubes chip and fall off the body. [Look. I am broken up and made into meat chunks,] the uterus says. [But it is more than that. I am empty and so I have gone to the shop to see if I can find the scraped out parts that were thrown into a dead bin.] It opens a drawer and pulls out a plastic bag filled with innards. [Here are my parts. But I don't know if they will fit back in,] the uterus says. It parts its engorged uterus and shoves the entire bag inside. It zips the edges and leaks.

The uterus pretends it is not a uterus. It walks in circles, flaying itself with each revolution. Hungry men beat their chests while the uterus sticks glass into its sides and cries citric acid tears. [I think I am ready for the garbage pit,] it says. The uterus runs again. It clings to the flat underside of a water glass. ((((((You Tear Us!)))))) it wails. The uterus braids its coils. The uterus sings a song. The uterus goes into a fit of rage and destroys a sink with its bare tubes. [I hate everything,] the uterus rages. [I want to eat porcelain and spit up raw material. I hate all these things. Make them go away. Make them forget that I ever had anything to do with them. I am not a uterus. I am just a thing. A bag. A sack. A piece of paper. A slice of flesh. Do not look at me. Do not remember that I ovulate. Because that is far from the point. Because I do not need to remember my fertility to be happy. Once, there was something inside of me but I could not bear the pressure it forced on my bowels. So I let it go. I opened up and let the thing slide out of me. Goodbye, thing. Goodbye. Adios. I do not want you within me. Because as much as I am a uterus, I am not a uterus. I do not want to sustain anything that is not myself. Call me selfish if that is your wish but I am just skin and there is nothing wrong with me. I pick and choose what I want residing within me.] The uterus strikes a man with a pair of paper scissors. The neon-colored handles stick out of his chest. [I have been stabbed by this double blade,] the man says. Implicated, the uterus runs away. It runs upstairs. It runs in a building, then out into a street. The uterus is scared. The uterus does not know what to do with itself when it is most hungry. It leans over and lets the little things that live in the gutter eat off its uterine walls. [I hear the uterus is living on the radiator drain, the uterus is making out with the faucet thing. The uterus coats its walls with Vaseline,] the men say. [Goodbye,] the uterus says. [Because I took a hacksaw to my old thigh bone, they say bad things about me. Because I did not want to feel another puddle sliding down my backside, they gossip about me. I am not the bad thing. I am not the same nurturer found in the holy family. I am one with the savior's mother. I am a thing that does not follow protocol. Do not make me breed.] (((((the uterus)))) ((((((will not breed with us))))) ((((((the uterus))))) (((((will not be bred))))) the men protest. It does not need to. The uterus keeps its blood to

itself and stores lactation in a glass jar for safekeeping.
[My milk,] the uterus says. [It is hermetically sealed. No
one can get at it now and years from now, when I feel the
most nurturing, I will unscrew this lid and drink everything I poured inside.] The uterus shrieks. It swallows
knives. It swallows scissors. It sticks its ovarian tubes
into a blender and pulses them five times—zap, zap, zap,
zap, zap. [Now I am a uterine smoothie,] the uterus says.
It sips its own juice and spits the chunky substance into
the nearest sink. [This is disgusting,] the uterus says. [It
is heavy with clots and old placenta. I didn't think there
was supposed to be any pregnancy hormones stuffed
into those eggs but I was wrong. And now my cysts suffer.] The uterus puts its eggs in milkshakes. [Better, but I
should add some of the cream that I stole from the men,]
it reflects.

[Holy uterus, mother of god, let us pray,] the eggs
chant. [Let us give up prayers.] [Let us pray to the walls.]
[Pray to the walls and their joints. Pray to the tiny mother flowers inside the tubes,] they pray, their egg shell
foreheads cold against the floor. [My tubes,] the uterus
responds. [My tub of tubes is near burning point.] [Boil-
ing point.] [Burning point and my mother burns herself
on my sides.] [Where did the uterus go?] the men plead.
[The uterus was here. The uterus was there.] Suffering
from their cries the uterus screamed into a blind reflection, then scratched its ovaries out. [The cysts lie,] the

uterus says. [Do not listen to their complaints. They erupt within the pelvis and cause internal bleeding. Because they are mean. Like little beasts or gremlins. I'd rather them be mythical. Then I can keep my womb locked and not fear anything.] [Fear everything. Or fear nothing,] the uterus cramps. The uterus leaves its waste products inside underwear drawers. [Underwear? Or under where?] There used to be a lover that was known only by his penis but even he became tired of such an identity. So he turned his penis into just a scrotum. Then the testicle merged into the sputum before disappearing. The uterus is alone. It is alone it is alone it is alone. The uterus sits on a stoop. The uterus resides in a pile of poop. The uterus. Always the uterus. Sad uterus. Teary uterus. The uterus sits in the center of the bone. Remember the song. [The womb stands alone, the womb stands alone. Hi ho the fallopian tube, the womb stands alone.] The womb cries. The womb dies. The uterus is all alone. [Uterus.] (((((((((()))))))))) [Uterus.] The uterus is a circle. The uterus is a square. Uterus here, uterus there, uterus everywhere. [I wish I may, I wish I might, live inside a uterus tonight,] the eggs chant. Uterus. (((((((((((uterus)))))))))))) [Hello? Uterus?] [Hello... uterus.] [HELLO UTERUS.] they scream. [Ignore the screaming,] the uterus says. The uterus too has a loud voice. It can drown out the eggs, but it doesn't need to. The uterus has other, more pressing things to deal with. The uterus does not

know how to control itself. The uterus does not understand contraceptives. This old uterus knows a person
who should not be with another person but both these
people crowd around the uterus and poke at it until it can
no longer breathe. [Breathe, uterus. Breathe,] it whispers
to itself. The uterus stares at the wall. The uterus is a wall.
The uterus contains a wall. [Hello, uterus. Do not go into
that sad sack. Do not do not do not,] the men coo. The
uterus is all alone. [Hi ho, uterus,] the radiator clangs.
Even with all that iron, the uterus is alone. The uterus
must atone. But first the old penis lover—the one that
became a scrotum, then disappeared as testicles. First
deal with that being, then deal the uterus. Because the
uterus is neither the first nor the only one with faults. The
penis doesn't know when to stop. First the penis needs
to be controlled. Pray, uterus. [Pray I may,] the uterus
prays. The uterus prays daily. The uterus prays nightly.
The uterus rubs its bed parts against a mattress and
wishes it might know divine words. [Goodnight, uterus. Goodbye,] God says. The uterus bleeds. And bleeds.
And bleeds. And bleeds some more. And bleeds until the
uterus is dry. Dry uterus. Dry and crumpled. Dry and
cracked. Dry and dry. Dry uterus womb cyst. This uterus
prays and prays all day. Until the uterus comes home. Or
until the sputum drills a hole in the wall. Not the egg. In
the endometrium. That is riddled with tiny blue worms.
Within the uterus.

Armed with scissors, a needle, and thread, the uterus paints its body parts blood red. [I am full of menstruation,] the uterus bleats and grows horns out of its pelvic area. An ax head pokes out of the center folds and the uterus takes care not to let its tubes run against the sharp ends. [I refuse to hack myself to death,] the uterus says. It cuts through an old bathroom mirror and watches the shards collect in the sink basin. [Leaf basin,] the uterus asks. [No, sink basin.] It sticks its tubes out and licks around its outside. A bitter taste makes the uterus shiver. [I am puckering,] the uterus says. [I am puckered up and cannot make any sense of my bones. Do I even have bones? Look, I am poking myself and there is no calcified resistance. I am an invertebrate! Look, no bones.] The uterus throws itself down on a sidewalk and stabs its center with the needle repeatedly. [Scissors, scissors on the wall. Scissors, scissors for us all,] the uterus sings. [I think I will cut my fallopian tubes with these scissors.] It snips and saws and cuts. The tubes fall off. Steam escapes from its ends. The tubes shrivel up and sprawl flatly on the ground. [Dirty things,] the uterus says looking at its tubes in disgust. It coughs up blood clots. The clots splatter on the floor. The blotches resemble dead body chalk outlines. [Who commits suicide,] the bovine uterus asks. [At least it wasn't me.] It chuckles. It lifts the tubes off the floor and swings them at a window pane shattering the glass. [Seven years bad luck? Or double that time in bad ovulation,] the uterus asks with mock glee. It eats the glass. Thick blood runs down its uterine walls. [I wish I had legs,] the uterus says. It salivates. It splits each tube in half and stares at the little almonds housed inside. [Are you people,] the uterus asks, shelling the nut and scooping a seed couple out. The seed couple quivers. [There was a garden in a deep shell but now it is razed, burned to the ground and so we are homeless,] the little female says. Its voice buzzes. The uterus lifts the female up and flicks her away. [I don't like your sounds,] the uterus says. [I find them annoying. Like neon light buzzing in my ear. Go away. Drown for all I care.] It turns its attention on the male seed. The little gnarled man clings to the seed shell. His head moves back and forth. The man sees the scissors and leaps onto the blades. [I'm free,] the man says. His head hits the joint between the blades. The scissors slice his skull open. The man falls to the floor. [That was unwise,] the uterus says. [I thought you would know better than to leap onto sharp objects. Silly thing. Where is your little Eden woman now? Don't you realize that the entire garden was just one large womb stuffed with flowers? This is the first time you have ever left.] It strips the peel from the man, revealing the solid muscle inside. The uterus waves the tiny seed man around in the air. It flings his ligaments onto the tiny buildings. Bittersweet meat stench envelopes the uterine walls. [Ugh, I hate this smell. It is too much like an abattoir,] the uterus says. [And if you think I don't know what an abattoir smells like, think again. Because how else do you think this uterus stripped from that cow of a woman?] It slits the man throat, cutting him in half.

Men ride the uterus to conquer new lands. They sit inside the uterus. They hang onto the uterus's outsides. [Do not drop us,] the men cry and the uterus shambles forward, tubes and ovaries swinging back and forth in a pendulous motion. The uterus slices her bowels open and the men topple onto the ground. They stick their heads into the dirt and move their arms and legs around. [We are flying,] the men shout. But they are not. Creatures with spider limbs walk up their backs and eat their spinal cords. [We have lost our vertebral qualities,] the men shriek. The uterus lies in a warm bath. It moves its tubes around, creating a whirlpool. [I hope that you have chlorinated this water properly,] the uterus says. [I do not want any bacterial growth to come upon my tissue. I can't shed those algal remnants. I scrape the parts clean but the hardened flesh hurts too much.] The uterus drinks the water up and spits it out from its rear orifice. The men shriek in its throat. [Let us out,] the men yell. [Let us go free. Now we are just little amoeba figures. We can barely breathe.] The uterus climbs onto a cactus and pretends the thorns are individual trees. The men cry. They bleed out. They push their feet through the uterine walls and leave puncture wounds all over the uterus's inside parts. [Stop trying to make me go into labor,] the uterus says. [I do not want you to hurt me like this. I have told you a number of times that I have no desire to push anything out.] The uterus picks nails out of its tissue and discards them in the desert wasteland. [I have taken over fifteen kingdoms without breaking a cyst,] the uterus says. It grunts as the men push out of the tube pits. [Can you conquer some other parts in our names,] the men ask. [We want to feel like we have accomplished something on our own instead of riding your coattails. Don't forget that we have the penises and you are just the vessel we choose to travel within.] The uterus sticks tongue depressors into its holes and scrapes them around the entrance. The men fall off the walls. The uterus hits its tubes against its chambers and listens to the hollow echoing. [Oh my,] the uterus says. [I am prolapsing. But what else am I supposed to establish? All I have is a bloody shoulder blade.] The uterus stretches out on the floor. The bovine uterus hisses and sobs. It pushes silt around its neck until it is completely rooted in place. [I am just a cow,] the uterus says. It pauses and the sand shifts. [Actually, I am more like a sheep,] it shrugs.

PART FOUR

MY TESTOSTERONE

A Radiator Play

RADIATOR:
Mewl, say I. Or mew. Or drool. I do not know the difference between my sounds and there is a beast rattling my pipes but let me ignore him in case that is enough to make the teeth dissipate.

ME:
Who says that fangs are like air and can just disappear because you will them to with the trophy tongue you hang from your navel in lieu of the penile apparatus you wish you had been endowed with?

RADIATOR:
Because you are just a woman, you do not know that I am simply a man trapped in metal and the longer I breathe, the more the steam is drawn out of my lungs.

ME:

I should be a mermaid then. You can cook my fish parts in the indirect heat, then you can use my female parts for the sex act I am certain you will not be able to complete.

RADIATOR:

But I am incapable of ingesting anything laden with mercury poisoning and you are very nearly some sort of thermometer. I am already filled with rust and other things that reek of the elemental nature of life but I refuse to enhance that nature to the extent that a little girl like yourself will crawl free of a tombstone and gnaw me with her genital teeth.

ME:

I am that little girl, but the teeth are not tucked between my legs like you think but pushed into the flesh of my knees so that when I crawl, I am able to bite the ground and even stone learns to fear me. But those teeth in my knees are just one end of several hungry bits merging with my digestive system. Help me crack my back and I will rid your spine of its rusted parts. I am the only girl you will ever leave with—though you will be tucked around my neck and spewing oil while I walk.

RADIATOR:

All the same, I once knew a woman who looked like
you.

ME:

Yes, but she was not me.

RADIATOR:

She could have been you. But the floors kept crumbling
around her and when I looked at her again, her head
was in the center of a wall and her lungs were swept
up beneath the carpet, then her fingers tapped out the
minutes until my death. But despite all her incessant
tapping she died before me, and it is a sad sound that
still haunts my pipe holes.

ME:

Do you mean pipe holes or penile holes? Perforated
margins or pencil punches?

RADIATOR:

Whatever you want to call them, they were holes of
flesh that should have rusted over but instead stayed
soft, warm, and wet while I beat my shoulders against
the floorboards and waited for the tiles to swallow me
up. For now, watch me bleat like the sheep I should
have been born as, then pretend like you don't see me

when I am taken away to the radiator slaughterhouse where I will be reduced to my most valuable parts and forced to watch as all the extra sinew is tossed away like simple rubbish. That is not the way any piece of metal should ever be treated. But I am fine with your watching me since it is the only way I can get my daily dose of meat into my diet—if only my pipes would not shudder so violently when I shake my legs.

ME:

When I menstruate into your face rust comes off my uterine walls but so does all that clotted tissue and the more that a man whispers my name, the more I imagine a lifetime locked in a lupine embrace with him and it is terrible to think of a beast instead of a sad hairless figure like you. But sometimes I dream of fucking all the ghosts and their bodies are hungry. All those entities can call my name.

RADIATOR:

They call me radiator.

ME:

They say you. They say me. They say us. But me.

Bluebeard's Wives

[Consumption!] we scream. In the dark, exchanging outside with the inside, we break our wrists and leave our
hands in the musky closets to fester on the shoe shelves.
A man with a bluebeard walks around, his spine sticking
out of his throat, swallowing a waxy moon umbrella. The
waxy moon grows in his bowel dumpster. The bluebeard
man eats a hanger. He swallows a toe. He swallows a shin
bone and opens his throat up. [Do you feel the splintered
ankle in my throat,] he says. He pokes at the pushed up
bone. He opens his throat and reaches inside, gripping
tiny bone thorns. The bluebeard man with the splintered
ankle pulls himself into a splintered chair and rocks on
the hymnal legs. [Prayer joints,] he remarks. [Rosary
bowels.] In his prayers he runs into the realm above in
which the living frees the dead. [This is no different from
the realm in which the dead free us,] he says. [Do you
hear the shining on their bell faces? The rot cannot com-

prehend the garlic bulbs growing out of their emptiness. And it all comes across their faces and leaves red streaks. Scarlet curses. Gray jinxes. But most of all, beware of that eternal syphilis.] Running to the nearest opaque window, Bluebeard, as he is now called, bursts through and removes each sagging wife from the inner panes. [Promise to lick me,] he says and the wives' mouths droop, drooling in anticipation. They stick their tongues out and the dead muscles hang against their chins. [Every solidified union is another lie,] Bluebeard says. [You cannot trust them,] he says of his wives. [You cannot trust anyone as long as the door remains unlocked.] [Come here, dead ones,] he coos. He reaches beneath the bed and removes the pale dead ones, who swipe their rotten claws at his hands and cut his palms in half. Bluebeard cries loudly. He makes a mess on the floor and his tiles run rampant. [I feel like I am bleeding but I think it is just another lie,] he says. Furious Bluebeard spits red. Bluebeard touches the sides of his head with his finger. [We keep forgetting that all these glorious things belonging to the blackest antennae. My wives were like mothers. Even with their radio silence, their cresting white waves of electric currents. Stop judging the stove top when the oven is barely hot enough to suffer the shallowness of some oceanic mess. Blistered is nothing. I can't stand how the closet door stays open when I sleep at night. Don't you realize that there are too many things stuffed inside the closet that want to bite me,] Bluebeard says. Angered by his wives' insolence, he skewers his eyelids and tears the thin skin off. He throws the eyelids onto the floor and like a child jumps up and down on them. [Every eyelid is just another collapsed bridge. Whether by bacteria or amoeba or piece of skin, or sinew, or gristle, or fat things, it is all the same. Stop talking about the length of your muscles. This isn't obvious when we keep running in squares and ovals to get from the bathroom to the crawl places below. For all I care, the gnomes in the walls can remove their faces and bite our chins with their solitary front teeth,] Bluebeard says as he eats burnt yellow sunflowers and sticks red and purple daisies up his nose. [Are my veins really pink,] he asks and blows his nose until his legs thicken around the thigh sauce. The bluebeard man soaks in a vat of vinegar grime. [Hustle these alley warriors,] he says. [I have wives to bite into submission.] The bluebeard man gropes his throat. The bluebeard man lifts and tucks. The bluebeard man is all alone. [Did you find the plastic sink in my knees,] he asks. He squeezes his mouth out. He fills five hundred wine decanters with his wives' skimmed fat and each yellow drop singes green.

A Man With a Hat

A man with a hat comes close to me. He waves until my snake-like hair wraps around his wrist, and he says, [I like the way your skin smells, now give it to me.] The man with a hat also has a badge which he waves around like a beauty queen or a beauty king (because this man does not like to get his genders mixed up). He pokes my upper arms until my skin bruises. [A badge equals the law,] he says. I work on unfastening my skin as fast as I can but my fingers keep slipping so that I end up un-buttoning one, then I slide past another five to unbutton the next. With so many buttons still clasped my skin has trouble opening. It should come apart like Velcro but my skin is fastened shut, clotted up with crazy glue chunks. The man with the badge puts his tongue in my ear and whispers [Stop taking your time and just give it to me.] Impatiently I tear my skin and it rips into long ropes. I twirl the skin around like paper streamers, tossing the homogenous coloring into the air while the man with a hat gathers up the pieces that hit the floor. [What will you do with them?] I ask but the man with a hat doesn't answer. The man with a hat doesn't care because he is a man with a hat and a man with a badge. A man with both a hat and a badge doesn't need to worry about what to do with the things that he collects. He just needs to worry about polishing his badge and keeping spinach out of his teeth. He knots the skin around his neck and soon my knotted skin looks like cystic lumps protruding from his throat. He becomes a walking tumor. I'd rather be a tumor than a naked skinless woman but I'm not lucky like that. I am all red flesh, cut up and mutilated, and everything I touch gets coated in a slippery layer of my blood. There is red on the walls and red on the bed and red on the street and red everywhere. This is because the walls and the bed open onto the street. Or maybe I have it wrong and the street runs through the bedroom. Either way, my bed is the hatted man's jurisdiction as given by the integrity and history of the law. The man with a hat and a badge puts his tongue into my ear again, swirls it around, and moves it away, sighing as his saliva soaks into my naked muscle. It is a cold night and the cold is even colder because of my skinless nakedness and I wish I could wrap a blanket around my red parts but even as I reach for the blanket, the man with a hat says, [I want that blanket.] He flashes his badge again. He smiles with a loaded gun pointed at my open gut, and he puts his tongue back into my ear. I thrust the blanket at his chest and the hatted man wraps the blanket around his shoulders, knotting it just beneath the jutting flesh that he stripped from me. I shiver and the hatted man pats my skin. His hand goes through my muscle, shredding ligaments and leaving a mess of knots and strings attached to the underside of his nails. Sometimes, he dips his hand too low and it penetrates my interior parts. He pulls his fingers out, sucks them clean, and pushes them in again. The hatted man tells me that I am his addiction, his compulsion. He continues to twist his hand around as he grabs at my skin. He snags a necklace off my dresser. He does this so quickly, I can't think of the point in time where he shifted from between inside my body to outside my body. The necklace dangles from his hands. [But that was a gift from my mother,] I say and the hatted man puts the necklace in his mouth. [Now it's mine,] he says and pats his stomach. The necklace makes a soft snaking sound in his gut. [What else do you have for me,] the hatted man says as his badge gleams in the harsh synthetic lights. His mouth is too wide and he keeps the gun trained on my right breast, as if he might blow the nipple off just by releasing a jagged breath. [This might all be easier if he just shot me through both my breasts,] I think and I want to whisper, oh, I want to whisper, I really do want to whisper even if the sounds won't come out, I want to whisper, [Do you want to take my uterus, too?]

A Room of My Own

There is only enough room for me. You will have to sit elsewhere. This room isn't connected to anything. It hovers in its own space, distant from roots. It defies gravity. While I am inside, I defy logic. I hang out the window and float instead of drop. You knock on the door but I do not have to answer. There is no sound here. Nothing you or anyone else can identify. I am alone. I prefer this. Once, you and I made love. It was a regular occurrence. We would reach for one another in the dark. Sometimes we would cry. It felt good but I thought I was being chained down. There was not enough room for the two of us. You said I was wanted but I did not want to be. I wanted to be left alone for as long as you knew my name. You did nothing wrong. Everything I hate about you is another thing I despise in myself. You were a good person. You are a good person. I should be left alone because I am neither. I am good at being alone. I am good at hiding

. STAR JASMINE .

in corners and crying. I need this solitary room so I can hide beneath a desk and weep until I sleep. You never liked the sound of my tears when you were beginning to snore. It was no one's fault. I always wanted to bruise my pillow until the feathers spilled out.

I thought it would be enough to love you. But there was no space for you. Not in my private room. I thought I could arrange a couch so you could keep yourself against a wall. Then we could spend our lives together. But I was wrong. I didn't know what I was thinking. The couch would not fit through the door. I could have cut the frame open with a saw but I didn't want to damage anything. I didn't want to breathe in sawdust just because you felt compelled to stay close to me. I didn't need you that much. I think you do not understand me. [We are people,] you say. [We must be surrounded by others. We can't spend our lives in a single room. You have to be willing to talk and be surrounded.] But I am surrounded. I am surrounded by walls. I can talk to them if I choose. They don't say much though. Sometimes, they nod or shake their corners. But usually, they are quiet. I speak and they listen. The walls and I are fine with this arrangement. I keep them company and they keep me safe. They enjoy the sound of a human voice. [I love you,] you say. [Why do you want to leave me?] Because I am better alone. Because a room cannot disappoint me. Because there are little spider-legged things bumping around within me and I do not want you near me when they escape. They are hungry and will eat everything. You, me. I would rather they eat me quickly and spare your bones. Their bites are painful. But I am not afraid of their fangs. I will laugh as they gnaw. I will show them your picture and taunt them. They will not eat any bit of you because I will keep you away.

Fine. Let us be metaphysical. There is no room. There is nothing but a couch floating in midair. But what does that mean? The silver coil no longer anchors me. You come at me with a pair of scissors. You try to sever my subconscious from my anatomical self. I kiss you and slide into the asbestos-filled corners. You cannot reach me there. Your lungs cannot handle the threat of plastique insulation inhalation. So I stuff myself into crawlspaces that run along the sides of the room. I do not mind the walls pressing in against me. The plaster tastes good in my mouth. I chew it and the concrete crunches. You stick your hands in my mouth and I bite them off at the wrists. You do not taste as good as the raw materials. I wear the fiberglass like a jacket. I smear it over my skin. I plait it into my hair. I shove it into every body cavity. You try to touch me and your limbs swell to three times their original size. I drift into the air and spread my torso across the ceiling. See, being metaphysical brings us nothing.

This room has a skeleton. The desk is the brain. It

charges the walls. The walls emit a bright blue light and move in circles. I sit at the top of my spinal column. It appears that I am just one of many vertebrae. But I am not. I am the master of the bones. And you are a mound of fecal matter. Get out of my room so the bones and I can rejoice. But you do not leave. You plant yourself on the doorway and cling. You are calcium and marrow. You are stubborn. You are a fungus. You are a blue-green thing that births dust spores. I am clearly allergic to you. When you touch me, I sneeze. Then the bones fall from my face. They land on the floor, askew. Some pile up in the wrong directions. I swallow the bones. You do not understand how much I need the bones. They give me structure. They keep my head from hurting. The room rotates on my shoulder blades and my arms open up to reveal sacred windows. I stick my head through the entrance and let the glass panes fall shut on me. I have a severed head. But you cannot have it, though I know that you want it. You say that you will take anything that I can give you. But all the broken things are mine alone. I fail at sharing, even the broken things, despite loving you. If you became a single femur, I might love you better. I might even be able to give you the chair beside me to sit on. But becoming a bone would remove your face and body. You would simply sit there motionless. I would have to move you around. It wouldn't do you any good. I promise you that. Because while you want to share in my space, sharing isn't enough. You want to experience it for yourself. You hate the idea that I have memories where you never exist. If I could, I would store you in a drawer and lock the entire desk. You would thump around, begging to come out. But I wouldn't let you. Just as I won't let you sit in my room now.

There is a ghost. It looks like me. It sounds like me. But you can tell the difference. The ghost is supposed to distract you but when it touches your arm, you run away. You only want my fleshy self. But my flesh and blood doesn't want you. You ask if I am dead. I am not. I won't lie to you. Not unless you want me to. Then I will tell you the truth because I never want to give you anything you want. The ghost pretends to sit at the desk, typing, writing stories and staring out the glass-less window. It beckons you towards it. I sit in the closet. I keep a thick wool veil over my face. I can't see through the fabric. I hope you can't tell it is me in here. You approach the ghost, then back away. The air around her is too cold. Your body temperature drops twenty degrees and your skin turns dark blue. You shiver and sink into the floorboards. You ice over. I cannot leave you to freeze. I climb out of the closet. I crawl to you. I breathe over your skin until you melt. Then you grab me. The ghost pulls you off. It gets between us. Chilled again, you press your back against the wall and wait for the spirit to retreat. I cry. The tears harden on my cheeks. I flick them away. They shatter on the ground and cover the plaster. The ghost holds my hands. She guides me back into my little room in the corner. She resumes her seat at the desk. She does nothing but pretend to stare at everything.

Daily, I think of dying. Always in a painless way though. Sometimes I do not mind the pain and other times I do. Sometimes I am allergic to everything. To you. To the room. My hands rub together, are sweaty and cold, and I break out in a rash. Think of the children who are allergic to water. How their bodies are constantly trying to kill themselves. I think I would like that. I am like that. But I do not like my situation as it does not hurt me. It simply leaves me disfigured and disappointed. The spider things keep trying to break out of my stomach shell. They crave meat. I slam my hands in drawers to keep them still. They do not know anything about the word NO. Someone said the spiders would be good companions as they are low maintenance. They take themselves for walks. They hiss when things get too noisy. The problem is that they crave the skin of their keepers. Like the monster in movie that wanted to eat its parents. How ironic was it that the entire time, the parents took turns having a late-term abortion only to have the monster born still? Then tried drowning the three-year-old monster but it survived. Then the eighteen-year-old monster was circumcised without anesthesia. I remember that in the movie it was always crying. Just like me. I am always crying but I lack the monster's chicken legs. Instead my body is formed normally. I am certain that is part of the problem.

The court system would like me to make judicial decisions from my room. I can't even decide if I should allow a chair into my room so that someone else can sit, let alone decree that a man should be jailed or even killed. I could always say the innocent are guilty. Then they could be jailed and alone. Everyone should be alone. It is safer. You can trust solitude. But still, it can drive you crazy. Being alone, it is hard to trust yourself. When I look out the window, strangely shaped mammals fly by. They drop out of the clouds and make a beeline into the body of water in the distance. I do not like the stingers that emerge from their tails. The appendages whip the air with a loud cracking sound. I think of the stinger puncturing my flesh and I cringe. When they catch me looking, many of them swoop my way in an attempt to bite me. They cannot get me through the glass but the threat is enough. I want nothing to do with them. I also want nothing to do with me. You shouldn't either. All you want is a simple couch so you can sit close. But I cannot give that to you. It is not that you don't deserve. You have done so much for me. You have been there for me for so long. But I cannot give you that little thing. There is no room for you here with me. If we are so close, even if we are just in the same room, we will inevitably touch. Then I will hate you. I hate everything that touches me. Even the walls keep their distance. The floors and the ceilings do so as well. They touch me only when I touch them first. I stay on a chair so they cannot accidentally brush against me. When the poison barbed animals outside bang against the window, I cannot hear them, because to me the glass is soundproof. Nothing can reach me. The animals spell out your name in blood. They want me to know that they know about you. They want me to think they can get to you. But they can't. They are only in my head. That is why so many of them have my same face. We blink at the same time. We open our mouths the same way. We are hideous beasts. I try to hurt you when you aren't looking. You feel nothing. I'm guessing that I don't hurt you hard enough.

Someone might think I am crazy. I am not. I am completely sane. There is nothing crazy about hating everything and insisting on a good amount of distance. That is why so many people live in white rooms. It is safer for them there. They know no one can touch them. Then they get their drugs and feel safe again. They are smart. If I could, I would join them. We could all cry ourselves to sleep together. But separately. We would not want anyone thinking we are ready to be a part of society again. Because that is not true. Not at all. I would tell you not to visit. I would sit by a large bay window alone and contemplate breaking my body against the glass. Sometimes, my room has large windows. Other times, they are small. I stick my head through the opening and the frames are either too loose or too tight around my neck. Often, I can barely pull my head back in so I am forced to stay in place for longer than I should. The animals come to get me. The spider creatures bubble around in my chest and threaten to break out. If they emerge then, I will have no chance. I will be devoured in record time. There won't be any binding string. Just me and my desiccation. I am tempted to offer you a couch. To let you sit. Just for a few moments. Just so you can understand my room. Even though I don't think you ever will. You do not know what this room means to me. You think I only want to leave you. But I think of terrible things all day. I want to protect you from them. Sometimes, when you are asleep, I think of cutting you, because I want to know what will happen. These are not normal thoughts. I can barely survive. I feel guilty saying I love you when I want to cause you so much pain. You deserve better. I should give you a couch to make up for all those thoughts but then, if you are right behind me, I will keep thinking them. So many horrible, bloody things have the potential of happening in my room. You are just one of them.

I think of death on a daily basis. I want to die. But not painfully. Not with any amount of blood. You tell me to live for something. To live for you. I know what I will live for. My room. That is all. That is all I have. A room and interior spiders and poisoned beasts flying around outside. I cannot live for anything else. I've tried. But the knife was calling. And the razors. And the rope. And the gas ovens. And the vials of poison. All of them. And they were delicious. I lived for them. You would only watch. Once, I went out west. I rode a horse through a bone cemetery. There were wolves lurking in the rib cages. A bear gnawed on a collection of pelvises. A bird of prey tucked several spinal cords beneath its tail. They all snapped at my feet. The horse ran because it was scared. It looked forward and I stared back, horrified by the animals chasing us. They were hungry. Dead meat hung around their mouths. Their teeth were red. Later, before this room, I went into a basement. I thought of time warps and sink holes. I sat in that basement and lost myself in piles of brittle, musty antiques. Porcelain dolls stared at me. Once, my basement was infested by porcelain dolls. Both the blinking and unblinking kinds. They tried to bite me. I thought I could let them stay but they knew how much I hated them. I knew they would wait until my back was turned. They understood the window. So I smashed them against the walls until their porcelain heads cracked. I kept their eyes however. I am not a terrible person. All those pairs of eyes were carefully stuffed into my desk drawer. I open that drawer up from time to time and the eyes look up at me. Their pupils roll around like white paint balls. The mouths lost to the basement walls still scream my name. I like my new room better. You shouldn't witness a mess like that. Hence why it's good that I stay alone.

I will be a floorboard for you. You can walk over me. Then I will shift or crack and make you fall. I do not mind nails sticking through me. They offer texture as I sit. Then I can remain in place for much longer. I put up mesh screens. I place them all around me. You stick your face against the nylon wire but cannot push through. Your face is too big for the tiny holes in the mesh. I am free. I have my little box and you cannot join me. I pity you. You do not understand my claustrophobia. If we are stuck in the room together, there will not be enough air for the both of us. I will run out of air. It will hurt. The asphyxiation. The heart burn. If I turn into the desk, will you put pressure on me? If you sit with me, you will break me. And broken, I can't be with you. Then you will be alone. Isn't that the opposite of what you want? Though, in thinking about it, that might not be a bad thing. The room would be preserved. If I cannot be in the room alone, then it might as well remain locked and abandoned. I know that you don't like the look of cobwebs but I welcome their ambiance. I will fit myself through the keyhole and return to the desk to write. You cannot lose the weight as quickly as I can. I will stop eating and wither away until I am able to slip beneath the locked door. I tell you goodbye through the key hole, but knowing you, you won't believe me. This room is mine. Even the dust particles are mine. I collect them on my skin and love their filmy weight.

I am a nervous person. Everything in me twitches. When I feel pressured, the spiders inside me bite as hard as they can. They poison me from the inside out. My eyes turn red and my limbs yellow with jaundice. You cannot see the discolorations as clearly as I can. They fade, then darken my pigmentation. Sometimes I look darker. Then I look bright white. It is not a good look. I am either ethnic or albino. The yellow makes me sick. When I forget to close the window, creatures come in to suck the melanin out. I feel faint during the process. Sometimes I actually do faint. Other times, my eyes just roll around in my head. (Do you remember when we used to make love at exactly one in the morning every night? We reached for one another without realizing. Sometime in the middle of the act, I woke up fully and wanted you off. I never pushed you. I never told you that I wanted to be free of your weight. I simply lay still and let you work until we were both done. After you fell back asleep, I sat in the dark, dripping with body fluids, and hating you. I wanted to hold a pillow over your face to stop you from breathing. Often, I went into the closet and sat on the floor, my head surrounded by coats and pants. In the morning, when you woke up, you would come to find that I had left the bed. I would be gone. Disappeared. Vanished.

You would worry for hours until I finally walked over to you. You never knew where I came from.)

I keep all the locks drawn all the time. No one can get into my room without permission. Not even you. I do not care if you are standing outside beating on the door for hours while I sit huddled inside. You will not get in unless I want you. The spiders from inside me crawl around freely. They make webs in the corner of the room in the shape of your face. I do not want them to eat you. I prefer you whole. If you were not whole, then I would mourn. Maybe not you. But I mourn something. A loss of identity, perhaps. Loss of all I've ever known. I have been making this room in my head since I was a child. Let me describe it for you. It is a single room. Four walls. A ceiling. A hardwood floor. A desk directly in the center. No part of the desk touches any of the four walls. The legs of the desk taper so that they only touch the ground in the slightest way possible. Before I embraced technology, there was a stack of journals in the center of the desk and many fountain pens. None of the journals overlapped the edge of the desk. There was always good light. Then I learned of typing. Someone mentioned it to me. First, I tried a typewriter but I made too many mistakes. I mashed the keys and they stuck together. And once I had written a word, I couldn't correct it when it was wrong. Then I found a computer. I loved it. I put it in the center of the desk. It is always part of the room now.

There are books in one corner of the desk so that if I am tired of writing, I can read them. These are books on various subjects. I stack them from largest to smallest—like a book pyramid. There is a chair. A high-backed chair with a cushioned seat so my hips do not hurt after many hours in a seated position. The walls are all bare. There is one window, just to my right. The door is to my left. I am alone in this room. There might be space enough for a couch but I am hesitant; I never imagined that my room would have a couch. Instead I leave the room as it is. It has bright white paint on all the encasing walls. There are no other adornments. There are no pictures in frames. There are no photographs. There is nothing. Just me, my desk, my window, my writing instruments. All the drawers but the one with the doll eyes are kept empty.

You cry in front of me. You want to be a part of my room but I do not know if I can do this. You should not spend your life according to someone who has always dreamed of being alone. You do not understand. My aunts all hanged themselves. My grandparents submitted to electric shock therapy. My parents have each been institutionalized. My uncles were shot with used guns, and none of them had children. I am all that is left. I am alone. I do not have genetics on my side. I am the last jar into which all this genetic material has been poured. Do you understand? These feelings of needing to be alone are a part of me. They are part of my makeup. They make me who I am. [You can be something else,] you say. [You can break the mold. You can free yourself. You don't have to let those things dictate who you are.] You say all of that. But you don't really know. You don't really understand that I want to be the way that I am. I like having that as my history. It makes me feel different. It makes me feel whole. I want to be tortured all the time. I want to hear voices and faint without warning. I want to be afraid. I want to be afraid of you. Of those thoughts that I have about you in the middle of the night. Of the terrible things that have happened to my family. Of myself. I want to know that my room will give me the solitude I need. You cannot give that, only my room can.

You say all you want is that little bit of space from me. But that means I am taking away from my own to accommodate you. That defeats the purpose. If I want my own space, my own room, I cannot allow anyone else in. Because then it isn't my own space. It is ours. [What is so bad about just having our space,] you ask. You do not mean that in terms of [we need space] — the plural speaking for the individual. You mean our as in [our]. As in a shared space. A space I am uncertain I want to be a part of. [All I want is a couch,] you say. A couch is a big investment to me, not because of expense but because of space. It means you will be taking up the space of an entire wall. That is a wall I cannot converse freely with.

If I let your couch through the frame, I cannot speak to the inanimate objects as freely. I would have to talk to your couch instead of just the wall. I imagine that you will want me to spend some time addressing you as well. I don't have the time or patience for that. The point is, as it always has been, my own space. So I can be alone. Without you. Completely unabashed solitude. If I let you in, I know that you will get hurt. The spiders will bite. I will stab you in the fleshy part of your thigh with a fountain pen when I hear you breathe. The pens that I keep at the center of my desk. Just be prepared for that. When you accept that. When you accept the vision of yourself covered in my bloody pens, then I will give you your godforsaken couch.

·Bleeding Heart·

Previously Published

Stories in this collection were previously published by the following presses/journals:

Excerpts from "Organ Meat is Killing Me" (originally "Organ Meat, Killing Me") by Turtleneck Press (chapbook) and Keep This Bag Away from Children.

"Men, Eggs" published by Menacing Hedge.

"The Body Forest" published by Danse Macabre Du Jour.

"A Room of My Own" published by THE2NDHAND.

"In the Vinegar Realm" published by scissors and spackle.

"Lilith's Extra Rib" published by A capella Zoo.

"Pickled Churches" published by Zymbol.

"A Man With a Hat" published by Loud Zoo.

"A Radiator Play" published by kill author.

Excerpts from "The Uterus Dies" (originally "The Bovine Uterus") published by Mixer Publishing, Resist!, and Shuf Poetry.

Acknowlegements

Special thanks to the following presses in which the stories in this collection first appeared: *Turtleneck Press, Keep This Bag Away from Children, Menacing Hedge, Danse Macabre Du Jour, THE2NDHAND, scissors and spackle, A capella Zoo, Zymbol, Loud Zoo, kill author, Mixer Publishing, Resist!,* and *Shuf Poetry.*

Thanks to Charlie, Katerina, and Badger for making this collection a reality.

We hope you've enjoyed the story. Please help us share this story with other readers by letting us know what you thought with a review on either **amazon.com** or **goodreads.com**.

Thank you kindly,
Montag Press Collective

Alana I. Capria is the author of the novel *Hooks and Slaughterhouse* (Montag Press, 2013) and the chapbook *Organ Meat, Killing Me* (Turtleneck Press, 2012). She has an MFA in Creative Writing from Fairleigh Dickinson University. Capria resides in Northern New Jersey with her husband. Her website is http://alanaicapria.com.